# FOREST OF REGRETS

Alexis Forrest Mystery

Book 6

## KATE GABLE

Byrd Books

# Copyright

fiction, which have been used without permission. The publication/use of these trademarks is not authorized, associated with, or sponsored by the trademark owners.

Visit my website at www.kategable.com

Join my Facebook Group:
https://www.facebook.com/groups/
833851020557518

Bonus Points: Follow me on BookBub and Goodreads!

https://www.goodreads.com/author/show/
21534224.Kate_Gable

# About Kate Gable

Kate Gable is a 3 time Silke Falchion award winner including Book of the Year. She loves a good mystery that is full of suspense. She grew up devouring psychological thrillers and crime novels as well as movies, tv shows and true crime.

Her favorite stories are the ones that are centered on families with lots of secrets and lies as well as many twists and turns. Her novels have elements of psychological suspense, thriller, mystery and romance.

Kate Gable lives near Palm Springs, CA with her husband, son, a dog and a cat. She has spent more than twenty years in Southern California and finds inspiration from its cities, canyons, deserts, and small mountain towns.

She graduated from University of Southern California with a Bachelor's degree in Mathematics. After pursuing graduate studies in mathematics, she switched gears and got her MA in Creative Writing and English from Western New Mexico University and her PhD in Education from Old Dominion University.

Writing has always been her passion and obsession. Kate is also a USA Today Bestselling author of romantic suspense under another pen name.

Write her here:
Kate@kategable.com
Check out her books here:
www.kategable.com

Sign up for my newsletter:
https://www.subscribepage.com/kategableviplist

Join my Facebook Group:
https://www.facebook.com/groups/
833851020557518

Bonus Points: Follow me on BookBub and Goodreads!

https://www.bookbub.com/authors/kate-gable

https://www.goodreads.com/author/show/
21534224.Kate_Gable

amazon.com/Kate-Gable/e/B095XFCLL7

facebook.com/KateGableAuthor

bookbub.com/authors/kate-gable

instagram.com/kategablebooks

tiktok.com/@kategablebooks

Also by Kate Gable

**Forest of Regrets**
**Forest of Deception**

**Detective Charlotte Pierce Psychological**
**Mystery series**
**Last Breath**
**Nameless Girl**
**Missing Lives**
**Girl in the Lake**

## About Forest of Regrets

**When a father vanishes with his two-week-old daughter, leaving behind a frantic wife and their eight-year-old son, forensic psychologist and FBI agent Alexis Forrest** is called in to investigate. The man's blood-stained truck is discovered abandoned on a dirt road, but there's no trace of him or the baby. As Alexis delves into the case, she uncovers a tangled web of secrets and lies.

With the serial killer responsible for her sister's death now behind bars, Alexis hopes for a fresh start in the small New England town where she grew up. However, peace is hard to find. Alexis tries to move forward and begin a new chapter with Mitch, her high school flame and the owner of a cafe/bookstore in Broken Hill. Yet, some wounds refuse to heal easily. The serial killer still awaits conviction, and the man wrongfully convicted of her sister's murder needs to be freed.

Haunted by the echoes of her past, Alexis races

against the clock to unravel the truth of the missing father and daughter before another life is lost. Is the father responsible for their disappearance, or did something far more sinister take place?

*Suspenseful and full of thrills, Forest of Regrets is the latest book in the addicting FBI mystery series from bestselling and 3-time Silver Falchion award winning author Kate Gable.*

*Scroll up to grab your copy today!*

# 1

# Alexis

It seems like the happier I am, the harder it is to leave the warmth and comfort of home in favor of rushing to a scene like the one I'm preparing to investigate. The information passed on to me by Special Agent Childs runs through my head like a ticker as I approach. A young father of two missing from his abandoned truck. A two-week-old daughter, also missing from the vehicle.

The possibilities are endless, and none of them are very positive. I have to remind myself not to let my imagination run wild, but my years of experience make that a challenge.

There is a cordoned-off area around the truck, and already a handful of local uniformed officers take pictures and notes. A soft growl sounds in my throat as I watch in the moments before climbing out of the car. I can only hope they haven't compromised the scene. They know better, sure, but I would much rather have gotten a first look before they started investigating. If only for the sake of having the best chance of the scene being as pristine as possible.

Then again, the sight of a shivering woman standing beside a minivan tells me the scene might not have been pristine in the first place. An officer questions her—I can't hear what they're saying, but I see the way she shakes her head almost violently in denial of whatever question was asked. From where I parked my Corolla, I can make out the silhouette of a child inside the vehicle. The wife and son, most likely. What are they doing here? Did she contaminate the scene?

Stepping out into the cold, damp air, I'm reminded of how much warmer it was down in North Carolina not so long ago. I have to zip up my heavy jacket against the dampness—some habits die hard, and this is no exception. Years of being told I would catch my death if I'm not careful. One of Mom's favorite mantras.

I make a beeline for that minivan, prepared to introduce myself. The closer I get, the more I can take in. The woman's eyes are red and puffy, her nose runny, her chin quivering. It looks like she threw her coat on over a pair of pajamas. Either she's a passing motorist who found something shocking, or this is the wife and mother of our missing pair.

It's the latter. "I'm telling you, Ryan would never do something like this." There's a fierceness in her response to the officer taking notes. Anger, even. Her emotions are running high, understandably so. She has a newborn involved in this.

"My name is Agent Alexis Forrest," I explain,

instinctively softening my tone to counter whatever this woman might be facing from a male officer. She might respond better this way. "I've been called out to help with the investigation."

Her eyes almost bulge and for a second, I'm sure she's going to lunge at me out of desperation. "Please, find my husband and my baby. This is a nightmare. I keep feeling like I'm going to wake up." She covers her face with her hands, her shoulders shaking as she sobs. A glance inside the minivan reveals a little boy playing on an iPad, though it doesn't look like he's having much fun. Distracting himself, more like.

When I look to the officer, he murmurs, "Jessica McAllister. We called when we found the truck. She showed up with her son, Ethan."

At least a hundred questions are rattling around inside my skull, but for now I murmur, "I'll take a closer look at the scene after I speak with them." It's clear from the way his brows knit together that he disagrees. No big surprise there. Local PD doesn't typically enjoy the appearance of an FBI agent at their crime scene.

When we're alone, I ask Jessica, "Can I get you anything? There's a gas station a couple of miles down the road. I could pick up coffee, maybe hot chocolate for Ethan?"

She shakes her head and wipes her eyes with the heels of her hands. "I keep telling myself I'm going to wake up. This is all just a nightmare."

"I can only imagine."

"I shouldn't have brought him out." I can only

imagine she's talking about her son. "It's just … as soon as I got the call that they found the truck, I had to come out here. They gave me the location and I just got dressed and bundled Ethan into the car and that was it. He doesn't need to be here, seeing this."

"I'm sure if I were in your position, I wouldn't want to sit on my hands at home." Of all times for Maddie to come rushing back in my memory. Not that she's ever very far away. Mom could hardly stand to be at home the first few days, always insisting she should be out there, searching. At the same time, she was always waiting for a phone call to tell her Maddie had been found safe and sound.

The torment she must have gone through. It was difficult enough to witness as a child, but as an adult, I understand it on a deeper level.

Thinking back on that makes me ask, "How old is your son?"

"He's eight. He adores his dad. He loves being a big … a big brother …" Covering her face with her hands, she releases a choked sob. "Where's my baby? She's got to be hungry. I haven't nursed since last night."

"Can you give me an idea of the timeline?" I ask once she quiets down a little. From where I'm standing, this doesn't make much sense. Why would he take the baby out? It was so cold last night. A nursing newborn would have been better off staying home.

"What do you mean?" she asks in a thick voice.

How to ask this gently, without judgment? "What

was the reason your husband went out with the baby at that time of night? Is she sick?"

Confusion passes over her face before she shrugs. "I honestly don't know. I was exhausted and I needed to sleep, so Ryan told me he would handle Isabel when she woke up. There were a couple of bottles already prepared in the fridge. I went down hard. When I woke up, they were both gone. He didn't leave a note, he didn't answer his phone when I called. I was frantic. This isn't like him. I swear, this is not like him at all." Like she has to convince me. I would probably feel the same way if I were describing something like this to a complete stranger.

It does seem very odd that the parent of a newborn would mysteriously take the baby out in the middle of the night. Was there some sort of emergency? Why wouldn't he wake Jessica up to let her know he had to go? Her sleep was important, but was it important enough to bundle up a two-week-old and take her out? And what about their son? What if he had woken up needing something? None of it makes sense.

I need to study the truck. That is the most pressing thing. "Why don't you do this for me," I suggest. "Are you well enough to drive? I could have someone escort you home. But I do think that would be the best place for you right now—for both of you," I add, since bringing up her son might shake a little sense into her. There's nothing she can do here that will help in any way, and he belongs at home instead of watching his father's truck be carefully studied for any clues.

She barks out a dry laugh. "What am I supposed to do? Sit around and hope? Go to the baby's room, maybe? Wait for her to come back?" Every word takes her a little closer to the edge, and now it's clear she can't drive herself. It's also clear she cannot be here.

"Is there anyone you can call to come and be with you? Family? Friends?"

"I don't know." She runs both hands through her light brown hair, then nods. "Yeah, I guess so. I just don't know what to do."

"I understand, but that's why we're here. We are going to do everything we can to find both of them, I promise." Time is of the essence. I can't bring myself to say that out loud. There are already enough horrors running through her mind at a time like this.

For the next couple of minutes, I busy myself with securing an escort for Mrs. McAllister and her son. "I am going to visit you as soon as I finish up here," I promise her as she climbs into the passenger seat so a cop can drive her home.

All at once her hand shoots out and grips mine painfully tight. "Please. Find them. My baby. My poor baby."

She's weeping softly by the time I close the door. Ethan leans in from his seat and awkwardly pats her shoulder. My heart breaks a little for both of them. I know what it's like to witness a parent's pain and not be able to stop it. Grownups are supposed to be strong, on top of everything. This is probably his first time observing his mother as a simple human being.

I really hope his world doesn't come crashing down the way mine did.

## 2

## Alexis

Once the minivan has pulled away, I pull a pair of latex gloves from my jacket pocket. I rarely go anywhere without them. Pulling them on, I duck beneath the caution tape that borders what has all the earmarks of a crime scene. The truck's door hangs open. The vehicle itself sits at a slight tilt, with the passenger side wheels resting on an incline along the shoulder of the road. Like Ryan stopped in a hurry.

The heavy clouds overhead don't allow for much light. I use my phone's flashlight to give me a better understanding of the truck's interior, the state it was left in. "The baby seat's still inside," I hear one of the officers murmur in passing, like they're trying to catch me up. It takes conscious effort to tune them out—I am not trying to view this through another professional's eyes. I want to form my own opinions.

Right away, it's clear there was a struggle. "Anyone notice this?" I ask, crouching beside the open door, a bit of torn fabric caught and hanging from the bottom corner. From a shirt or a jacket? It's blue plaid, from the looks of it. And if it was caught here, at the bottom of the door, that tells me the person whose clothing it came from was on the ground at the time. There was a struggle.

Of course, the blood on the steering wheel has already hinted at violence. There isn't much of it, just a smear, but that's officially one hundred percent more blood than there should be on a steering wheel at any given moment. "Have we gotten any prints from this?" I ask as I carefully study every inch of the black leather. It's a little worn, like Ryan drove it a lot, but aside from the blood it seems he kept the interior remarkably clean. That makes any abnormality stand out in even starker contrast.

"No prints in the blood, but we did get a sample," someone calls out nearby. Meanwhile, I use a pair of tweezers to pull the torn fabric from where it got caught and drop it into an evidence bag.

There is, indeed, a baby seat in the back facing the rear window. Inside is a pink and white blanket that looks handmade. "Let's check this for any hair not belonging to the family," I announce, slowly and carefully removing the car seat for it to be taken into evidence. "I want it checked for blood, too."

Once I'm satisfied with the truck's interior, I begin searching the area around it, bent at the waist. At first, nothing stands out but what might be present on any random roadside, bits of broken glass, gravel, nothing out of the ordinary.

Until I jump back at the appearance of what looks

like a muddy footprint leading away from the truck, positioned close to the truck's grill. "Let me see the bottom of your shoes," I bark to the first officer I see. They look nothing like the heavy tread pattern on the ground. A pair of heavy soled boots made them.

"I need photos of these," I announce, pointing at the three clear prints which soon fade to nothing. The mud must have worn off. I take a big step over the prints, then shine the flashlight on the ground close to the passenger side door. It does look like someone might have walked here recently, but it could have been the first people on the scene for all I know. The ground is disturbed, there are no clear prints from a boot. A few patches of old snow nearby tell me the ground might have been muddy enough for a pair of boots to pick up.

I'm too frustrated at what seems like incompetence to be here a minute longer. Once I've confirmed there are no other signs of a struggle nearby, I asked for Jessica's address with the intention of heading over to question her. By now, the sun is starting to break through the clouds, giving me hope the day won't be too rainy and gloomy.

Not that there's anything particularly pleasant about what I have to do next. A two week old baby. What would it be like for a mother to go through that? She's freshly postpartum, still recovering, probably already dealing with a roller coaster of emotions as her hormones fight to balance out. The pain must be so intense.

The family lives in a neat, trim home on the

outskirts of what looks like a pretty neighborhood outside of Bangor. Jessica's minivan is now in the driveway, parked in front of a single car garage attached to a two-story home whose white walls and black shutters give it a striking appearance.

Right away, I notice the lack of another car parked nearby, either in the driveway or at the curb. Maybe Jessica couldn't find anybody to be with her on short notice. I decide to ask her about it as I raise my fist to knock against the front door. A pretty wreath hangs on it, with a sign reading *Welcome* attached to the front.

Jessica flings the door open, wide-eyed and hopeful. "Did you find anything?" she asks before I've had time to take a breath.

"It's tough to say just yet." If she doesn't know about the blood, she doesn't need to know. She is already on the verge of breaking, it seems. I don't know if she's stopped crying since she left the scene. Her light brown hair is now in a loose ponytail, with strands hanging around her flushed face. "The forensics team will need to do a little more investigating before we can confirm anything. Can I come in?" I ask with a gentle smile.

"Of course. Sorry." She backs up to let me into a charming living room. Family photos and framed prints cover two of the walls—there's a beaming bride and groom, then a photo of the same couple standing in front of the Leaning Tower of Pisa. Another of them in front of Machu Picchu, from the looks of it. There are tons of pictures of what has to be Ethan at various stages. Isabel is too young to have earned so many places of honor. My heart clenches at the idea that she might not have the chance unless we work fast and get lucky.

There are also renderings of homes and other buildings interspersed with the photos. "Which one of you is the architect?" I ask, admiring them.

"Ryan. These are his favorite projects. The ones he's most proud of." With her arms wrapped around herself, Jessica joins me. "There are times when he disappears into his office and completely loses himself in whatever it is he's working on."

I turn my attention to the wedding photo, a full length professional shot of the two of them posed in front of a quaint little chapel. "You're a beautiful couple," I tell her, and she smiles. "How long have you been married?"

"Ten years," she tells me with a note of pride in her voice. Suddenly her brief smile dissolves, replaced by what might soon become a fresh burst of sobs.

"Let's sit down," I suggest, gesturing toward the cream colored sectional. There's evidence of a newborn all around – a laundry basket full of colorful onesies and blankets catches my attention. The socks are so tiny.

"I need to ask you some questions," I explain, slowly and gently. "Please, don't misconstrue them. I don't ask these things out of any suspicion or judgment. Any little detail might help us get to the bottom of this. Does that make sense?"

Her head bobs before she runs her hands over her

hair and tucks the loose strands behind her ears. "Sure. Whatever it takes."

"You've been married ten years. How would you describe your marriage?"

Her bloodshot brown eyes crinkle at the corners before she chuckles. "What do you expect me to say? We're great. Everything's great. We just had a baby. It's a little crazy, yeah, but … we've been happy. We've always been happy."

"Do you work outside the home, or are you a homemaker?"

"I teach fifth grade," she explains. "Though I'm currently on maternity leave. With my leave ending right around the time classes are out for the summer, I won't be back until fall."

She's lucky. Some new mothers are forced to go back to work right away. I'm sure she was looking forward to spending Isabel's first six months together. "And Ryan is an architect?" I confirm. "How would you describe the way his work has gone lately?"

She lifts a shoulder. "It's been fine, as far as I know. Challenging, but then it always is. There haven't been any complaints, though, if that's what you mean."

"What about any recent stress? Has there been anything out of the ordinary that you've been able to see?"

Bingo. For the first time, indecision touches her expression, making her forehead wrinkle. "Nothing that I know of," she tells me, though she speaks more slowly now. Carefully. "But … "

Seconds tick on the clock hanging in the middle of

the photos on the wall. Valuable seconds, critical seconds, but I force myself to remain silent while waiting for her response.

Releasing a shaky breath, she says, "He's been getting phone calls."

"What kind? Has he told you anything about them?"

"Never." She clasps her hands and squeezes them between her knees, taking another deep breath. "Once or twice over the past couple of weeks, I've heard his phone buzz but he grabs it and leaves the room right away. Random times, like ten or eleven o'clock."

I can imagine many wives having a serious issue with something like that, but many wives aren't going through the first two weeks of their baby's life. When sleep deprivation is involved, late-night phone calls probably take a back seat.

"But then a call came in three nights ago when I was nursing Isabel, around midnight. It seemed like a strange time for someone to call. What surprised me more was that he answered. I'm not sure he even realized I heard his phone go off—I was in the nursery, he was in the bedroom."

"Were you able to hear anything?"

She shakes her head. "No actual words, but I heard his tone of voice. He wasn't happy to talk to them, whoever they were. In fact, he sounded kind of angry."

"Did you mention it to him?"

"By the time I got back to bed, he was asleep. I totally forgot about it until now, honestly. There's been so much going on." Again, she touches a hand to her head, distracted now. "With the baby and everything. I'm only going on a couple hours of sleep most days."

"Completely understandable." This points to Ryan hiding something from his wife. A phone call at midnight? Immediately, my thoughts go to an affair, though Jessica says he sounded angry. He might have been angry that his affair partner would call at that time of night, while he was at home.

I have to wonder how that would translate to our current situation. It could be the affair partner is also involved with someone else, someone who learned about the deception and decided to take action. But that doesn't explain why Ryan took the baby out so late at night, unannounced, and with no message left behind.

No matter who placed that call, this points to the possibility Ryan has been hiding something. That's enough to warrant digging deeper into his life.

# 3

## Alexis

By the time I place a call to Agent Childs, hoping to catch him up with what I've discovered today, my head is swimming. At least I can retreat to the peace of the car, closing my eyes and resting my head while I wait for him to answer. I've been at this for four hours, according to the clock on the dashboard. Four hours in which I've received no updates from the field office or local PD on Ryan or Isabel. It's going to get cold again tonight. Is she at least being sheltered somewhere?

"Agent Forrest," he sounds roughly the way I expected upon answering the call, strained, frustrated, abrupt. "Give me the rundown."

"I've been talking to neighbors and friends for the past few hours," I report. "By all accounts, this is the perfect family. The perfect marriage, the perfect everything."

"Nothing is that perfect."

"Not according to everyone who knows them.

Jessica is everyone's favorite teacher, the one the kids come back to visit after they leave her class. She's extremely active in fundraising at the school, as well, and does a lot of volunteer work around the community. Mostly educational organizations, like the local library, though she also spends a few hours every weekend at the local food bank, stocking shelves and sorting donations." In other words, she's 'Superwoman'.

"What impression did you get of her?"

"I honestly have to wonder where she finds the time to do any of this. The house was incredibly neat, considering there was a baby born two weeks ago. Beautifully decorated. Although to tell you the truth," I point out, "the neatness could have more to do with Ryan than with Jessica. Apparently, from all reports, he is a very meticulous person."

"Who told you that?" he asks with a note of interest in his voice.

"Their neighbor across the street, Mr. Winkler, commented on how perfect the lawn and gardens always are. Mowed and trimmed and edged within an inch of their lives, he said. He once witnessed Ryan scolding their son, Ethan, for accidentally dislodging one of the stones they used to line the front garden. He said it was loud enough to hear inside his house with the doors and windows closed."

"Does he strike you as a tyrant? Domineering?"

"I didn't get a sense of that when I spoke to Jessica —there was no hesitation, no going over the top to convince me how great everything is. It could be he's just a particular sort of person. That would line up well with him being an architect. Very precise, detail oriented."

"Not the sort of man who packs up the baby on a whim and takes a road trip, in other words."

"That's about right. Jessica did mention a strange phone call a few nights ago. Ryan seemed angry at whoever was calling. She didn't get the chance to ask him about it."

"Could be he got one of those late calls last night," he reasons.

"And with Jessica two weeks postpartum, running on fumes? She was probably sleeping too deeply to hear the phone ring." The poor woman. Thinking she was getting a break, a solid block of hours to sleep, only to wake up to a nightmare.

I gaze up at the house, where I've returned after my hours of canvassing the neighborhood, visiting the people whose names Jessica gave me. Friends, mostly, though there were a few colleagues of hers and Ryan's.

"I'm going back in to ask a few more follow-up questions," I conclude, pulling myself together. "Their little boy was taking a nap when I visited earlier. He probably needed it after being pulled out of bed before dawn to race to the truck." That must've been so jarring for him. So confusing. I was almost asleep the night the police came to tell Mom and Dad that Maddie's body had finally been found.

I need to snap out of it. This is not the time to think about Maddie. Tyler Mahoney, the man who killed her, is currently behind bars. I was able to track him down after all these years so we can finally get the justice we deserve. Of course, there's still the matter of the man mistakenly convicted, the man whose name I want to clear, but I can't afford to give that much of my mental energy now. Isabel is out there somewhere, along with her father.

It's Isabel who weighs heaviest on my mind as I knock again against the black painted door with its cheerful wreath. When Jessica answers, I'm surprised to find her wearing clean clothes. Her hair is clean and brushed, and when she lets me inside, I see the laundry has either been put away or just moved someplace else.

"I'm crawling out of my skin," she explains, wringing her hands together. Instead of stopping in the living room, she continues through the house and I follow without saying a word. She seems distracted, lost in her thoughts.

"I need something to do, you know?" We reach the kitchen, which smells like lemon and disinfectant. "If I sit around, I'll go crazy. I'm afraid I'm scaring Ethan. He's never seen me like this." She picks up a sponge from the already pristine counter and wipes an invisible stain.

Gazing out through the back window and into the expensive backyard, I find Ethan sitting on a swing set. He's barely making any effort to push himself back and forth, staring at the ground while gripping the chains holding the seat in place. I've never seen anyone look so forlorn and lost.

"Can you tell me anything about him?" I ask. "What's his relationship like with your husband?"

"Oh, they're best buddies." Jessica's shoulders rise and fall as she takes a deep breath, then tosses the sponge into the sink. "I don't even know what I'm doing. Where are they? Where is my baby?" She hangs her head, softly weeping.

"I promise, we're doing everything we can." How empty that must sound to a grieving mother, a nerve-wracked wife.

"She's so sweet. Such an angel. She needs me," Jessica whispers.

I wish there were something I could say, but nothing short of telling her we found the baby alive and well will make a difference. "She's with her father," I venture. The thing is, I'm not even sure if that's true. The blood, the torn fabric, it could point to something much darker.

"That's what I keep telling myself. It's the only thing keeping me going." Then she sighs and looks toward the window. "And Ethan, of course. He's a smart kid. He is sensitive, he sees, and hears, and feels things some kids his age might not pay attention to. I want to keep him from as much of this as I can, but of course he's got questions. I wish I'd never taken him to where they found the truck, but I was operating on pure reflex when that call came through."

"Would it be all right if I go out and speak to him for a few minutes? Or we can bring him in so you can sit in on the conversation … " My mouth goes dry all of a sudden and I have to fight for my words. "I went through something similar to this when I was a couple years older than him. I wished the police who were working the case would've talked to me instead of looking through me."

"Oh. I'm sorry to hear that." She chews her lip and looks out the window again. "Sure, he might feel free to open up a little more if it's just the two of you. But I'll be right here the whole time," she adds, with a note of guardedness that I guess any mother would express.

It's actually a relief to step outside into the fresh air instead of inhaling disinfectant fumes. I take a few deep breaths while descending the back steps and cross the yard. It clouded up again during my interviews and now there's even a hint of snow in the air. Typical of early March, always a tossup.

Ethan lifts his head at my approach. "I saw you this morning," he informs me. "You were the lady who talked to Mom."

"That's right. And you're Ethan." He nods slowly. "What's your favorite thing to do, Ethan?"

"Play soccer." He didn't have to think about it.

"Are you on a team?"

"Yeah, we made it to the semifinals last season."

"Good for you. Maybe you'll do even better next season." Glancing toward the kitchen window, where I know Jessica is watching from the other side, I ask, "How are you feeling? Do you have any questions for me? Anything you're confused about?"

"I'm confused about everything." His nostrils flare when he breathes out a deep sigh. "Why did my dad go away? Where is Izzy? She's too little to be out here. What if she can't eat? Who would hurt my dad?"

Slowly, I lower myself into a crouch in front of him. "I know, there are so many things to worry about right now. And I am really sorry this is all happening. I am doing my best to find them—everybody is, I promise."

"We were supposed to play Minecraft this weekend," he murmurs, staring at the ground again, digging at it with the toe of his sneaker. "We were gonna make popcorn and get pizza and everything. I couldn't wait. What if ... " His nose twitches when he tries to hide his sniffles.

"You and your dad do a lot of stuff together?"

"When he can. He's always really busy with work, but he tries to hang out with me and do the stuff I like. When it's nice weather, we play soccer, or ride bikes or something."

"Sounds like you guys are really good friends."

"My best friend," he whispers. This time, there's no hiding the wave of emotion. A tear drips onto his clenched hands before I fish in my pocket for the travel pack of tissues I bring along with me for exactly this purpose.

He doesn't hesitate to accept it—no pretending he's too tough. I guess certain situations go above that.

For a while, I stay with him, letting him feel the way he feels without asking any more questions. For now, that's enough.

# 4

# Alexis

Someone is screaming.

The sound rips me out of a nightmare. Or am I still having a nightmare? I can't tell. I get out of bed, rubbing my eyes, only I don't know if I should go downstairs or stay here. Maybe I don't want to know what's happening.

But I have to know. My feet move quietly, so quietly–I've gotten good at skipping over the spots where the floorboards are creaky. I lift the door a little as I open it, so the hinges won't squeak so loud. Though right now, I don't think anybody would hear if they did.

"Where is she? What did they do to her? Where did they take my baby?" It's Mom, only somehow it's not. I didn't think human beings could sound like that. I flinch when something down there breaks. No, it shatters. "Why can't they find her?"

"They will." Dad always does his best to calm her down, only right now he doesn't sound very calm, either. His voice is shaking and he's struggling the way she is by the time I reach the top of the stairs and sit down. "They will. And they're going to find whoever did it. And when they do, I'm going to kill him whoever he is. But first, we're going to bring Maddie home."

There's a knock at the front door. At first, I'm not sure I heard it, Mom and Dad's voices overlapping down there. The second time it's louder.

I'm so cold all of a sudden. People don't show up at each other's houses at this time of night. It could be something bad. What if it's something bad? My heart's going to burst out of my chest, but I watch from the top step as Dad walks down the hall from the kitchen. I watch the back of his head—he stops as he reaches the front door and looks up the stairs. I don't think he sees me, hidden in the shadows, or at least he acts like he doesn't.

I grip the banister with both hands when the door swings open and there's a couple of cops on the front porch. Cops who look sad. They take off their hats before one of them says, "I'm very sorry, but we've identified the body as belonging to your daughter, Madeline."

Mom comes bursting down the hall, howling, and Dad catches her before they both sink to the floor, holding onto each other. All I can do is sit in the shadows and watch them fall apart before getting up like I'm in a trance. There's something sitting on my chest, so heavy I can barely breathe, can barely move. But I do move, I move so fast, running straight to

Maddie's room. Her bed is made up the way she left it that day, the last day, and I throw myself face down on it before screaming into one of her pillows. It still smells like her.

My eyes snap open all at once. It isn't Maddie's room in front of me, barely visible in the predawn darkness. It's Mitch's room. Our room.

Still, I look around, breathless, sweating. Waiting to hear Mom's scream downstairs. I would swear I can smell the shampoo Maddie used to use. It's right there, at the edge of my memory.

That terrible night. Of all times for it to come back to haunt me. Hearing Mom screaming, howling like some mindless creature. Howling over her lost baby. To this day, I don't think either of my parents know I was watching and listening that night. I told them I heard Mom crying and went to Maddie's room to feel closer to her. In a way, I guess that was true.

Now, I'm back in the present day, lying beside a softly snoring Mitch. The sound is comforting. Just knowing he's here lets me leave the nightmare behind. Twenty years have passed since that night. Yet it is still so fresh.

I feel sticky, clammy, thanks to the cold sweat that broke out over me while I was immersed in the horror of finding out my sister would never come home. I have to sit up and run my hands through my hair, getting it off the back of my sweating neck, turning the pillow over to the cool, dry side. Obviously, the nightmare was brought on by everything the McAllister case has stirred up. By the time I gave up for the night and came home, there were still no updates. Not so much as a hint of where Ryan might have ended up, and why the baby was with him.

It's Ethan I can't get out of my head. He's too young to understand he might be staring down the prospect of losing both his dad and his baby sister—and his mother, too, if that were to happen. The way I lost my parents, though they survived physically. There were years where I may as well have been an orphan. With Dad going to prison for attempted murder and Mom sinking deep into the bottle, into depression, then marrying a man she thought would be her salvation but who really drove a wedge between us.

It took time for us to rebuild. We're still rebuilding, the way she and Dad are tentatively rebuilding their relationship. We might be able to get our family back on track, but there's no making up for lost time. I can only hope Ethan doesn't have to go through what I did.

"Hey." I didn't notice Mitch's snoring, going silent. He sits up when he finds me on the edge of the bed, staring out the window. "What's going on? Are you okay?"

The man is magic. All it takes is the slight pressure of his hand against my back to untie all of the knots twisted up inside me. Tension drains from me like water from a bathtub once the plug is pulled. My muscles loosen and I almost slump forward when they do. It takes a moment like this to realize how tense I usually am. Especially when there's a fresh case like this.

"I had a nightmare," I explain, closing my eyes and sinking deeper into the relaxation he brings as his hand travels in slow circles over my back. He moves closer, and the warmth of his body comforts me. "It was the night they found Maddie. When those two cops came to the house. I swear, it's like I was right there. I can still smell her room. I can hear Mom screaming. Dad was crying and promising he would kill whoever did it."

"I'm so sorry." Sometimes it's what he doesn't say that impresses me more than what comes from his mouth. He doesn't tell me to put it behind me. That the nightmare is over now, the past is in the past. There's none of that. He lets me feel the way I feel without trying to force me through it.

"Do you think there will ever come a time when there is a case that doesn't somehow remind me of her?" It's an honest question. I turn my head to find him looking up at me, one arm bent behind his head as he rubs my back with the other hand.

He looks sleepy, his dark hair is mussed, but his blue eyes are as full of warmth as ever. "You work a lot of missing person cases," he points out with a gentle wince. "I can't imagine there being a time when you aren't reminded in some way of what your family went through. It worries me a little, so long as I'm being honest."

Since when do I not worry him? "If you're concerned I'm, like, torturing myself or something … "

"No, nothing like that. All I want is for you to be

able to heal, whatever that means for you. Some people would use the job as a way of processing their feelings, their grief. Others would approach it from the direction of setting things right. Getting justice for others that they couldn't get for themselves and their loved ones."

"I think I might be a combination of the two," I confess in a whisper. "What does that say about me?"

"It says you are the woman I love," he whispers back, smiling gently. "I wouldn't expect anything less. But you know, as much as you feel you have a responsibility toward the people you're trying to help, I would respectfully remind you of the responsibility you have to yourself."

"I know … "

"Not to me or your parents or anybody else but you. You need to protect your peace of mind, whatever that means, whatever it looks like. I'm afraid you don't do that enough—and don't ask me how you would, because I'm not sure, myself."

"But I should try," I conclude, nodding slowly.

"You should. Because in case you forgot, I want to build a life with you. I want a future for us."

"I want the same thing." No matter how much confusion I wrestle with on a daily basis, that is one thing I'm never confused on. Mitch has become my true North. My touchstone, my soft place to land.

"Good. Glad to know we're still on the same page." We're both grinning as he gently pulls me down until I'm lying beside him, my back to his front, so he can curl himself around me. "Come on. I scheduled a late morning at the cafe and have been looking forward to the extra sleep."

It doesn't matter to me whether I fall asleep again or not. If anything, it's much nicer to lie here, awake and alert, with Mitch's arm around me and his soft breathing close to my ear. I'm safe here. I'm home.

# 5

# Alexis

"Are you sure you don't need any help around here?" As I wait for Mitch to whip up two cups of his special brew, I have to smile at the inviting atmosphere he's created in his bookstore cafe. It's an ideal combination, and by the time we arrived around seven o'clock —hours after Mitch normally comes in to open up— there were a handful of customers reading the morning paper while drinking lattes and hot chocolate. Sure enough, we got a couple of inches of snow overnight, though the bright sunshine and slightly warmer temperatures this morning will probably melt it in no time.

"I have been looking for a little help behind the counter." He winks at me from back there, working the machine. "Though I don't know if you would be interested in the uniform I have in mind."

"Oh? A simple polo shirt or sweater wouldn't suffice?"

"I was thinking more along the lines of a short little dress," he explains, lowering his voice so only I can hear. "Or maybe a French maid uniform."

"Explain to me what a French maid uniform has to do with brewing coffee and serving pastries."

"You're right. I should save that for around the house." He winks, and even though I know I shouldn't encourage him, I can't help but giggle.

"I mean it, though." I accept a foamy latte to which he's already added sugar. "It's so … welcoming around here. That's special. Don't take it for granted."

"Believe me, I don't." He's not joking anymore, and now I see and hear the pride he has for his business. It's a pride he shows through the excellent work he does in the kitchen, baking bread, quiche, pastries. He figured out what he wanted to do, and he made it happen.

He also happened to build a wonderful little spot where people from town can come together, share a cup of coffee, discuss their favorite new books or simply sit with their crocheting while eating breakfast. There are three women doing just that, tucked in the corner of the café, and I sort of wish I was one of them. Not that I'm particularly crafty, not that I've ever been great at making and keeping friends. I have a hard enough time carving out attention and energy for Mitch, the person who deserves it most.

He joins me at one of the free tables, waving to a pair of customers as they leave with new books in hand. For a minute, it's enough to sit back and admire him in his element. He knows everybody's name, remembers many of their drink orders off the top of his head. It's not surprising. He has always been that committed to knowing me, taking care of me. Why wouldn't he feel that way about other people?

He catches me staring and arches an eyebrow, lips twitching. "What? Are you planning on running away?"

"Are you crazy?" I ask with a laugh.

"You're staring at me like you're trying to memorize my face. I mean, not that I can blame you."

I can't help but roll my eyes. "Maybe you should have an open mic night here once a week, since you're such a comedian. You'd have everybody rolling in the aisles."

"Don't tempt me. I've considered doing that, you know."

"Have you?" This is news to me.

"Not for stand-up comedy—though if someone wanted to give it a shot, I wouldn't stop them. But I have considered hosting something maybe once a month at the start. People can come in and play their instruments or read poetry or sing. I don't know," he concludes before taking another swig of his drink.

"I think that sounds like a great idea."

"What would your talent be if you performed?" he asks.

Tapping a finger to my chin, I pretend to think it over. "I could demonstrate self-defense techniques?"

"Oh, I'm sure that would have everyone riveted."

Leaning in, I murmur, "What if I did it in that French maid uniform you were talking about?"

There's a twinkle in his eye when he replies, "I might need you to demonstrate for me at home first. I need to vet the talent."

His soft, brief kiss tastes like coffee, but I'm sure mine does, too. There's something special about finding someone who makes you feel like you're the only other person in the world when they look into your eyes. Someone who gives you their full attention even in a room full of people. It should be more common than it is, finding someone like him.

The bell above the door chimes, and we turn as one to find a familiar girl strolling in. She recognizes me on sight and her already pleasant expression turns to a wide, beaming smile. "Agent Forrest!" Camille Martin approaches with her arms outstretched, and I happily stand to accept her hug. Camille was the reason I came back to Broken Hill all those months ago, after she was abducted by the man who murdered my sister. She was leaving a shift here at the café, walking home when he took her.

According to Mitch, she still has her bad days— more than once she's called out, too overwhelmed to show her face among so many others. But those days are fewer and farther between as she slowly recovers from her trauma. "Please, tell your parents I said hi," I offer, and she promises to do that before ducking into the kitchen to clock in.

"She looks good," I murmur, taking my seat. "Healthy."

"Yeah, she told me a few weeks ago her parents found a therapist she likes. Someone who specializes in that kind of trauma."

"I'm so glad." I can't help but think back to the therapists Mom and Dad sent me to during the madness that was the aftermath of Maddie's body being discovered. During the search for her murderer, during the arraignment and trial of Russell Duffy. I had already been through half a dozen doctors, at least, by the time Dad took matters into his own hands and shot Russell on the courthouse steps.

After that, Mom was understandably devastated to the point where searching for another therapist must have been too much for her to handle. There are some things I remember clearly, and one of them is the day I decided to study psychology. I wanted to know why I felt the way I did, and to maybe help other people going through the same chaos.

It seems like the longer I spend back here in my hometown, the more the past and the present insist on overlapping. Every day, there's something to remind me of that time. When it felt like the whole world was collapsing. Like I was screaming, and nobody could hear.

The idea makes me think of Ethan. I'm sure he woke up this morning hoping his dad would be home, or that at least he would've called. The way Mom was always waiting for someone to call.

"I think our quiche has cooled off enough by now." Mitch ducks into the kitchen and soon reappears with a gorgeous, golden quiche on a cake stand.

He only took it out of the oven when we first arrived. The aroma of cheese and onions reaches me and makes my mouth water. Within moments, he places a slab in front of me. It's still warm, studied with chunks of feta and spinach.

"You are too good to me," I declare before cutting off a bite and popping it in my mouth. My eyes close as a soft groan stirs in my throat. "But please, don't stop," I add before swallowing and going back for another bite.

He looks pretty pleased with himself after testing his own slice. "Not bad. Maybe a little more cheese. Should I caramelize the onions first?"

"I wouldn't change a thing," I insist around a mouthful. "I mean, why mess with perfection?"

"You flatter me."

"I mean it." I'm already halfway through my slice, too, and it was a generous one. "Here I was, thinking I couldn't possibly eat all of this."

"I figured you would need something hearty to get you through the day, since you have a bad habit of forgetting to eat when you're busy on a case."

Speaking of which … "I really should get on the road," I decide with a sigh. I've put it off long enough. "At least it's not too long of a drive, but I'd better get moving anyway."

"Here." Before I can go, Mitch leans over the counter and retrieves a paper bag from underneath, printed with the shop's logo. "For the road."

A peek inside reveals a ham and brie baguette— one of his new additions to the café menu—and three chocolate chip cookies. "Remind me to send you the bill when I have to replace all of my clothes with a bigger size," I murmur, standing on tiptoe to give him a kiss.

"It's a bill I would happily pay," he assures me with a grin.

# 6

## Alexis

My first stop this morning is a drive to the Portland field office, where Special Agent Childs reported there's mail waiting for me. Rather than have him forward it to Broken Hill, I head over to personally pick it up. I can check it out once I reach Bangor, where the local police chief has offered space in their headquarters. I was actually surprised that he was so quick to accept my presence. Some things transcend pride, and this is one of them.

Along the way to Bangor, I call the police department and am put through to his direct line. Chief Myers is gruff, but there's a teddy bear quality about him that reminds me of Captain Felch from Broken Hill. "We're negative for blood on the car seat," he explains, and the news leaves me grinding my teeth in frustration. Another dead end. "We're still waiting on an analysis of a few hair samples pulled from the blanket, but it's not looking good. Mostly the strands match the description of the parents and older brother."

My heart is sinking, but I do my best to play it off. "Thank you for the update. I should be there in another hour or so."

"I'll leave copies of the photos taken from the scene if you would like to review them," he offers. I almost don't know what to do in the face of so much cooperation.

"Thank you so much." Ending the call, I blow out a frustrated sigh. I knew it was a long shot, getting a hair from the baby blanket, but we don't have very much to go on. I can't believe nobody has seen or heard anything about these two. They may as well have vanished into thin air.

And how many cases have I covered in the past several months which involved something similar? There's always an answer. What a shame that it all seems obvious after the fact.

The chief was true to his word. When I arrive and step into the small office – just like in Broken Hill, it's tucked into the back corner of the floor – there are folders full of photos waiting for me. Closing the door, I remove my jacket and hang it over the back of the chair, then pull my laptop from my shoulder bag and set it up on the desk. It's not a very big desk. I might need to ask for a spare table if there are any. Otherwise, I'll drag a folding table in here if I have to. I need the space to spread out a little, or I will once the case picks up speed and there is more evidence to comb through.

Flipping open the top folder takes me back to the scene yesterday and the sight of blood on the steering wheel as I examined it. Now, I'm staring at photos carefully depicting the stains, which were beginning to turn a darker red color after exposure to air for however many hours the truck had sat open and empty.

Why would he be bleeding? There was no evidence of the truck crashing or striking anything on the road. A quick tour through the rest of the photos takes me to images of the truck's exterior, which wasn't so much as scratched. If there were damage, I could construct a narrative where Ryan was bleeding and confused and tried to go for help. In his confused state, he might have thought it was best to take the baby with him. A terrible thought, for sure, though it would at least make a tragic sort of sense.

But there is no damage.

Would it be likely for a carjacker to lie in wait on a quiet, unlit back road? What would be the odds of someone coming by? And no, a carjacker would take the vehicle. There might've been a struggle, sure, some reason why Ryan was bleeding. Then what happened? This theory is getting me nowhere.

There's another possibility. Was there someone in the truck with them? Someone Ryan might've picked up along the way?

Now, I return to the photos of the truck's interior. Is there anything about the passenger seat to point to a third party? Fresh dirt on the floor mat, maybe? No, nothing like that. The truck is in remarkably good condition except for the steering wheel.

There's something almost unnerving about poring over the details of a potential victim's property. Then again, that could be my history informing my current feelings. I learned a long time ago that there are two types of people in the world, those who are aware of terrible things because they watch the news, and those who know of those terrible things because they've experienced them. For a long time, my sister was a headline, a symbol in the press. Innocence lost, an American tragedy. For the people reading those stories, that was who Maddie was. A beautiful young girl with her entire life ahead of her and nothing but potential.

That was barely the tiniest fraction of the whole story. There were so many times I wanted to scream, to call in to radio shows and tell them exactly who my sister was and how much we loved her. I wanted them to stop talking about her like they knew the first thing. They only used her name to keep people listening and calling in.

I can't help but think about that now, going over the details of Ryan's life while reviewing my notes from yesterday and typing them up for the sake of adding them to what the team has already uncovered. Sadly, it's not much. There has to be something under the surface. Ryan might be a good father and a great architect, but that doesn't mean he's perfect. Hearing about those late-night phone calls planted a heap of skepticism in my gut.

I lean back in my chair, blowing out a sigh, reminding myself not to let my imagination run away with me. Still, no matter how many directions I try to approach this from, the existence of those phone calls keeps bubbling to the surface. It's all I have to go on.

Hours spent in the car, then sitting hunched over the desk, leave me stiff enough that I have to stand and stretch. When I do, I notice the mail sticking partway out from my bag. There are a few pieces of junk in there, along with a postcard from Detective Gladstone. The fact that he took the time to send a postcard from a little tourist spot near the beach makes me laugh. *Hope all is well and you aren't taking any foolish risks.*

"You and Mitch, both," I murmur, shaking my head. I don't exactly love looking back on the harrowing experience I went through down in North Carolina, but the photo of the beach at sunset makes me smile. Maybe I'll keep it as a memento.

The last envelope is printed with the name of a law firm in the top left-hand corner. Not exactly the sort of thing that makes me eager to open up and see what's inside. I tear it open before I lose my nerve to find a letter.

At the top of the letter, in bold print, are the words: **Efforts to Accelerate Russell Duffy's Release**.

All of a sudden, my mouth is bone dry. Before I read another word, I type the name of the law firm into my web browser. Their specialty is in advocating for wrongly imprisoned convicts, either providing their defense or funding it while raising awareness.

And they want to clear Russell Duffy's name.

*While it has been reported in the news that a man with possible ties to a series of murders in Broken Hill, Maine has been arrested, this does nothing for the man currently sitting behind bars for the murder of your sister, Madeline Forrest. While we understand nothing will bring her back, we hope on Russell's behalf that you can bring yourself to provide assistance in clearing his name.*

Beneath the body of the letter is contact information I'm free to use if and when I choose to.

Maybe I should've done more before now to help him. I should at least have reached out to him personally to let him know Tyler was arrested. I told myself I didn't want to get his hopes up, which is not untrue, exactly. The last I checked, Martha's Vineyard PD are still getting information from him related to crimes in the area. He could be dragging things out, biding his time, and that does Russell no good.

It's not enough that Tyler is off the streets, that he will never harm anyone else. I need to right this wrong. Russell has already lost so much, even though he has also gained the chance to make his life better while in prison.

He deserves to be free and to have his name cleared. I might not have put him behind bars, but I can help get him out of there. If anyone can do it, I can.

I need to. Not only for Russell, but for myself. Sitting on my hands and waiting for Tyler's arrest to result in something concrete isn't getting me anywhere. This way, I can still feel like I'm achieving something worthwhile.

For now, though, what I need to achieve is uncovering a lead in the McAllister case. I turn my attention back to the files and tell myself I can always think about Russell and Tyler and everything else on the way home tonight. I have enough driving to do, after all.

# 7

## Alexis

"I don't feel right doing this." I'm filled with doubt by the time I close the door to Mitch's truck. "I should be working. Those people are still missing. And here I am, ready to go on a hike?"

Mitch closes his door after pulling a picnic basket from the back. "We're having lunch together on a Sunday afternoon. The sort of thing normal people do. It's a beautiful day," he points out, waving an arm to showcase the blue sky overhead. Yes, it is a glorious day for mid-March, unseasonably warm. The sort of weather that reminds a person that spring exists. It won't be winter forever.

When all I can do is frown, he sets the basket on the ground and takes my shoulders in his hands. His touch is comforting but firm at the same time. "Your boss said it himself yesterday, right?"

"I shouldn't have told you that," I grumble, remembering Agent Childs' advice that I take a day for myself.

"You just came off an extremely harrowing situation back in North Carolina, and that nightmare in Martha's Vineyard." He sighs, rubbing my shoulders. "You need to take care of yourself. Even he sees it."

"I was only doing my job."

"Now, we both know that's not true." He is willing to give me plenty of space, but some things he clearly can't let go. "You had a very close call. Two of them, in fact, within days of each other. No one is asking you to take a sabbatical, but you do need to take care of yourself. Which means the occasional Sunday picnic lunch. I don't think it's too much to ask," he concluded, letting go of me and picking up the basket again. "Let's go. Get a little fresh air into your lungs."

Fresh air isn't the problem. Time is. Too much of it has passed without a single clue to point us to Ryan's and Isabel's location. I can't help but think of Jessica and Ethan, waiting. Hoping. "Is it all right if I at least login and do a little work once we get home?" I ask as we set off with Mitch in the lead. "A compromise, sort of?"

When he groans, I add, "Hey, it's not the same as making the drive out there and getting my hands dirty."

"Right, right," he groans before smirking over his shoulder. "I don't need an entire list of reasons why this is what you need to do. So long as I know you're taking time for yourself when you can."

Time for myself. It's still such a foreign concept. "I don't feel like I deserve time for myself," I confess. It's an easy hike, more like a walk, really, through the foothills along Broken Hill's northern border. The higher we go, the more of the town is laid out before me. I used to like to come up here back in the day— we both did, together, after we started dating in high school. It was the only time I ever felt peaceful, really, when I could sit up above the town. Away from the looks and the whispers and the pity. So much pity.

"You finally came to that conclusion?" He turns and offers me a hand to help me over a boulder jutting halfway out onto our path. "I could've told you that months ago."

"Well, if I were missing, I wouldn't want to find out the people looking for me were on a hike, ready to have a picnic lunch."

"When are you going to settle into the idea that you are not the only person working this case? You never are," he reminds me—still gentle, but firm. "You are not the last FBI agent in existence. There are dozens of people right now working the case."

"I know. But I've made promises."

"I know." He reaches back for my hand again, this time to stroke my knuckles with his thumb. "But again, not everything has to fall on you. Let somebody else handle things just for now."

Why is it so impossible? I want to be the person he needs me to be, because he is who I need in my life. He deserves a girlfriend with the ability to balance out work and personal life issues. He needs me to be here for him. He's always here for me. I just wish it wasn't so darn difficult to change my ways.

The sunshine is nice. I needed it. Grabbing a scrunchie from my bag, I pull my hair up in a ponytail, letting the warm rays hit the back of my neck. "Vitamin D is a natural pick-me-up, right?" I ask.

"One of the best there is, along with exercise. We're getting that now, too."

I'll take all the help I can get after spending half of last night thinking about the letter I received yesterday. I haven't mentioned it to Mitch yet, having come home late. I was so tired from driving and working and worrying that I didn't have the energy to go into it. That doesn't mean my subconscious gave me a break. Every time I started to fall asleep, I would think of Russell in his prison cell.

"I got a letter yesterday," I blurt out once we're around halfway to the spot where Mitch and I used to sit together when I needed to hide from the world. It didn't surprise me that he remembers those times, or that he would want to visit there now. "It was sent to the field office. There is a group of lawyers working to clear Russell Duffy's name, and they want my help.'

He slows his progress, not saying anything at first. Finally, he sighs. "I was wondering why you were so restless overnight."

"I'm sorry. And there I was, thinking I would spare you."

"For the last time." He stops and turns, facing me while wearing a frown. "I don't want you to keep things from me, or to spare me, or anything like that. You didn't really spare me anything, did you? I practically needed a Dramamine after all that bouncing around you did."

"I'm sorry. I wasn't trying to keep anything from you long-term." When his frown doesn't ease, I fold my arms. "Am I supposed to report every single thing that happens to me over the course of a day, as it happens? Do you want constant texts? And what doesn't require an update? Do you need to know when I use the bathroom?"

"All right, all right." Shaking his head slowly, he turns his back on me and continues leading the way. "You've made your point."

"It's just that I know you feel like I kept too much from you in the past, and maybe I did, but that's over now."

"I'm happy to hear it." He does not, however, sound convinced. I guess I can't ask for miracles.

After another twenty minutes, we arrive at a clearing overlooking Broken Hill and the surrounding area. Lake Morgan sparkles in the distance, and when I shield my eyes from the sun, I can look out over the woods where Tyler Mahoney's cabin was discovered. The cabin where he held Camille Martin and where he might have held my sister. We're still not sure. There are so many questions.

Mitch sets up the picnic while I stare off toward the woods. Was she there all that time? An entire month of waiting and hoping, praying and crying, with our mother making emotional pleas in front of news cameras, begging whoever had taken Maddie to bring her home to the people who loved her. She was only a short drive away. Did she think nobody was looking for her?

I am so deep in my memories, my troubled questions, that the presence of Mitch suddenly standing at my back makes me jump a little. "Hey," he whispers, winding his arms around my waist, touching his lips to the top of my head. "Where are you right now? It seems like you're far away."

I am. I'm twenty years away. "If that were me," I whisper, my attention still trained on the dark woods which will soon burst into bright green life when spring finally arrives, "I would want the police or whoever was looking to never stop. All those weeks Maddie might have been waiting for somebody to rescue her, and nobody ever did."

"I know," he whispers, his arms tightening just a little.

I touch the back of my head to his shoulder. How can there still be all this pain in my heart? There's still so much from those days that feels unresolved. I don't know that any number of cases will make it go away. "So yeah, maybe I obsess. I want to do for these people what we couldn't do for her."

"You were a child," he reminds me with a sigh. "You couldn't have done anything."

"I know, but it doesn't make me feel much better. Nobody found her. I don't want anybody else to go through that—victim or family," I add. "That little boy needs his dad. He reminds me so much of me."

"And you aren't helping him or anybody else by driving yourself to the point of exhaustion." With one more squeeze, he lets me go. "Come on. Let's eat all of this before the bears decide to come out and see what we brought for them."

Not the most cheerful thought. "What do you think I should do?" I ask as we sit down on the blanket Mitch stored in his backpack. "I want to help Russell. It's the least I can do."

"So long as you aren't doing it out of some sense of guilt. I mean it," he insists when I try to wave him off. "You didn't do anything to put him in prison. As for helping him get out, absolutely, you should if you can. But don't blame yourself for incompetent police work back when you were ten years old and there was nothing you could do to change things."

When I open my mouth, prepared to protest, he adds, "And don't ever blame yourself for what your dad did. You know I like him. He's a great guy. But the choice he made to fire that gun had nothing to do with you. Right?"

"Right," I agree while unwrapping a thick sandwich. I can't wait to sink my teeth into, and not only because all that walking helped me work up an appetite.

"What do you think?" Mitch asks, watching me. He's been toying with the idea of offering sandwiches on the café menu, and this is one of his latest creations; prosciutto, fresh mozzarella, with a sour cherry spread and tons of arugula on one of his homemade baguettes. The flavors explode across my tongue and leave me closing my eyes, groaning happily.

"I think you are much too talented," I decide, leaning over to give him a kiss. "And I am happy to taste test any other ideas you have."

"You're so supportive," he chuckles before taking a bite of his own sandwich.

"Hey. I'm willing to make sacrifices."

# 8

# Alexis

By Monday morning, the energy surrounding the case is at an all-time high. There's a sense of urgency that wasn't there before, the sort of urgency that makes people desperate, going back over information in a last-ditch effort to find something they overlooked the first time around.

That's what I'm doing as I go back over the list of names Jessica gave me when we discussed the people her husband knows best, the ones who would be able to give me a clear idea of who he is and what he might have been up to in the days and weeks leading up to the disappearance.

A knock on the open door leaves me face to face with Chief Myers. "I wanted to let you know I got the okay from the state police to bring in the tracking dogs. The divers are still at work out there," he adds, referring to a small, man-made lake roughly half a mile from the spot where the truck was found. "They haven't brought back anything yet."

What a surprise. As hard as I try, there's no shaking off a sense of frustration at the news. "Well, we'll have to keep digging. I'm thinking about reaching out to Jessica McCallister and asking for additional names. I spoke with a couple of people who worked with Ryan years ago. I'm wondering if there's anyone he works with now who might be available. Someone to give me a clearer view of what was going through Ryan's mind those last few days, especially when it comes to those phone calls." They're still one of the only potential leads we've come up with. Why was someone calling him so late at night? Why was it so secretive?

A phone call to Jessica tells me she is in increasingly worse shape. "What does any of this have to do with what's happening right now?" she asks when I request the names of Ryan's colleagues at his architecture firm.

"I'm doing whatever I can to understand his mental state."

"Are you saying Ryan might be having some kind of breakdown?"

"Not exactly, but I also can't rule anything out," I point out as gently as I can. She's alarmingly on edge, and now it seems I've insulted her. "At a time like this, we can't afford to rule out anything until we've explored it. It could be he was going through something he didn't want to bring up – with the baby and everything, he might have wanted to spare you any extra stress. It's possible, right?"

She keeps me hanging for a moment or two before

she grunts. "Yes, I guess so. He does have a friend at the firm who he talks about sometimes. Work friends, you know, not the type who socialize or anything. Mark Darvish."

Having a new name to track down energizes me. A call to Ryan's firm gets me transferred to Mark's direct line. "I'm wondering if you have a little time for a cup of coffee today," I suggest, crossing my fingers. "I have a few questions about Ryan. Maybe you can help me, since I understand the two of you are friendly."

His response is immediate. "Yes, sure, I'd be glad to meet up with you."

"I don't want to interrupt your workday."

He chuckles without humor. "Are you kidding? No one's doing a lot of work around here right now. We're just waiting for the phone to ring with news."

<hr>

**M**ark Darvish is a man in his mid-thirties, like Ryan. The first word that comes to mind when we sit down together at a café in downtown Bangor, where Ryan's firm is located, is *precise*. His khakis are smoothly pressed, the collar of his long sleeve polo is crisp. He sits ramrod straight across from me, tapping his fingers against the table in a nervous rhythm. "It can't be possible that no one saw anything or knows anything. In this day and age? When everyone is connected all the time?"

"I understand what you mean," I admit. "I can't

tell you how frustrating it is, trying so hard to track down even the smallest clue."

"The baby ... " Pain touches his expression, furrowing his brow, making him wince. "We threw Ryan a little shower at the office. It was sort of a joke, you know?"

"How did he feel about the new baby? Did he ever speak about her with you?"

"He was thrilled. Really, over the moon. He's a good father, devoted to his kids. That much, I can say without hesitation."

Then why does he sound so unsure? Like he's trying to convince himself while convincing me. I can't exactly put my finger on it. I only know his response makes the skin on the back of my neck prickle. "Did you two ever speak about his home life? From what I've heard from neighbors, they sound like an ideal, loving family."

He's not so quick to answer this time. Instead, he stares down into his coffee cup, turning it in circles. "It's probably none of my business," he begins, and those six words have the power to make my pulse pick up speed. They are usually the precursor of something useful.

"Whatever it is, it can stay between us," I promise, ready to jot down whatever it is he has to say. At a moment like this, it isn't easy to not come off as some salivating ghoul, ready to pull secrets and exploit them. There's a fine line to walk, trust to earn.

"Lately, he's been different."

I knew it. I knew there had to be something. It's a challenge, keeping my voice even. "How so?"

"I've spent the weekend thinking it over. Trying to put a timeline together. Because as soon as I heard he was missing, the first thing that came to mind was how strangely he's been acting over the past couple of months." He lifts the cup to his mouth and takes a long gulp.

Months? My surprise must show itself on my face, because he nods. "Yes, it's been that long. Funny, but I never put it together before now. Sometimes, people go through things. We don't have to understand them."

"So it seemed to you that Ryan was going through something?"

"Not that he would ever come out and say it. He has too much pride for that. And he's not the kind of person who wanders around, spouting off personal information. I figured, live and let live. It didn't seem to be affecting his work, even if he was a little distracted these last few weeks."

"Exactly what has been different about him?"

"He's been moody. On edge. There is no telling which version of Ryan will come into the office from one day to the next. Days have gone by where he hasn't said a word to anyone from the time he walked through the door to the time he left."

"And that's not like him?"

Shrugging, he explains, "He's not what you would call social—you wouldn't find him gossiping at somebody's desk–but he's always polite and cordial. And I'm not the only one who's noticed it. Everyone has."

"Did he happen to mention any sort of personal issues? Something at home, something family related, maybe? Was it stress over the baby, do you think?"

"You know, I might have written it off that way," he admits, "if it wasn't for the phone calls."

Here we go again. "He was getting phone calls at work?"

"All the time. Eventually, one of the other guys cracked a joke. We were in a meeting and Ryan kept checking his phone like he was waiting for something. So, one of the guys we work with asked him if we were interrupting something. Just joking around, nothing serious."

He blows out a heavy sigh, shaking his head. "Ryan glared at him until the room went silent. He then got his stuff together and left. He walked out of the office without a word. No explanation. And that's not the only time he did something like that, either. He would offer up some half-baked emergency and we wouldn't see him until the next day."

None of this points to the happy, loving, husband and father Jessica described. It does, however, line up with what the McAllister's neighbors described. Especially the man who witnessed Ryan laying into Ethan for something trivial.

I have to phrase my next question carefully. "So pretty much everybody around the office witnessed this change in him? The way he's been acting?" He nods. "Did anyone have a theory about it, maybe? Did you get a sense of what might be behind it?"

"I mean, there was one thing that came to mind right away." He meets my eyes briefly, like he feels guilty. "Consensus around the office was, it seemed like he's having an affair. It's the most logical conclusion."

Yes, I agree. I keep my thoughts to myself, though, thanking him for his time, telling him I might have more questions later on.

Right now, it seems like questions are all I have.

# 9

## Alexis

"The more I learn about this guy," I tell Agent Childs on my way back to the police station, "the clearer the picture gets. He was hiding something. It could be Jessica genuinely doesn't know about it."

"It isn't like she didn't already have enough on her mind," he points out. "If anything, that would make things easier for him. Sneaking around while she was distracted."

I can't imagine it, but then much worse things have happened than a husband cheating on his pregnant wife. The idea makes my heart hurt for her—it's clear she adores him.

"That still doesn't explain the specifics surrounding our case," I groan, rubbing my temples while waiting at a red light. A woman crosses with a stroller in one hand and her toddler's hand in the other. She reminds me of Jessica, pretty, young, maybe a little frazzled, but holding it together. How much longer is she going to be able to hold it together, especially if she finds out Ryan was having an affair? I'm afraid I'm going to find out before long.

"No, it doesn't, but it gives us the impetus to dig deeper into what Ryan McAllister has been involved with. I'm going to recommend we pull financial records, phone records, anything we can get our hands on." The determination in his voice gives me hope. "Now, there's the possibility the man was hiding something big, something that put his life and his child's life in jeopardy."

It's an ugly thought, but it's the only logical conclusion. I hate to think what this will do to Jessica, and how I'm going to explain the need to dig into personal information without giving too much away. She's fragile, increasingly so, and there's still a little boy at home to keep in mind. Just like me, he doesn't have anybody else to lean on. I didn't meet Mitch until high school, and he was my salvation. An ear to listen, a shoulder to lean on. Ethan doesn't have that as far as I know.

Once I've finished filling him in, I promise to get back to him with any updates as soon as they come along. It isn't another few minutes before I pull into a guest spot at the police station and head inside. I'm sure the chief will be eager to hear what I've uncovered, even if we still don't have an idea of exactly what it means.

As it turns out, I'm not the only one with news. "Finally, you're back," he calls out from his desk when I pass his open door. I was planning on leaving my jacket and bag at my desk before heading his way, but it's clear he's in no mood to wait. "We just got word from a couple of the businesses in the area surrounding the McAllister home. They sent over their CCTV footage from the night of the disappearance. We might be able to track the route he took with the truck."

Instead of going to my office, I drop my bag and jacket on an empty chair and join him behind his desk. "There's a lot of footage to sift through," he admits. "Four different people cooperated with our request—so far. There could be others. For now, we have more than enough to review."

"We could divide it up," I suggest. "What are you looking at now?"

"This is from a camera mounted outside of a hardware store on Main Street," he explains. The black-and-white footage is crystal clear, with the camera trained on the intersection of Main and what looks like a major cross street.

"When I asked Jessica to give me an idea of the time she went to sleep, she said it was probably around ten o'clock," I recall. "So we should start looking at footage after that point in the night."

He adjusts the video progress bar until the time-stamp in the upper right hand corner reads 9:55. He plays the footage back at three times normal speed, and for a few minutes we sit and watch cars speed past. Not many—this is a commercial area, and from the looks of it, most businesses were closed at that time of night.

A flash of something dark and shiny crosses the

frame. "Go back," I urge, leaning in. "Was that a truck?"

"Looks like it," he confirms, taking the footage back a minute and playing it at normal speed this time. The silence between us crackles as we watch, waiting.

The truck comes up fast, flying through a yellow light to beat the red. It takes a little patience to pause the footage at just the right time, but before long, he is able to stop it at exactly the point where the truck was in full view of the camera. It's Ryan's, no doubt about it.

And he isn't alone.

"Is there someone sitting next to him?" My heart is in my throat and if I don't breathe, I'll pass out. For the first time since I got the call telling me about the disappearance, it feels like we found something real.

"Sure looks like it," he agrees. "All right. The truck passed through this intersection at a high rate of speed at 10:25. Let's see how long it took him to make his way through town."

Putting together a map based on the locations of the other businesses whose footage we obtained, we attack each location in order. One thing is abundantly clear when we catch the truck roughly a mile down the road from its first appearance, he wasn't driving that fast to beat the yellow light. He was flying flat out, careening down the street, taking a left-hand turn so sharply he almost went up on two wheels.

"And he had the baby in the truck," I whisper, troubled by the implications.

"Maybe the baby really was sick," the chief muses, exchanging a glance with me. "It could be there was an emergency with her."

"Why wouldn't he let Jessica know? And why not call an ambulance?" I add.

"Sometimes, people lose it in the face of an emergency. They don't think. They react."

Staring at the screen in the footage, which the chief paused, I mull it over. He makes a good point. There's never any telling how a person will react in a moment of high stress, especially when emotions are involved. There's nothing like a sick baby to send even the most levelheaded person into a panic.

"That doesn't explain why he's not alone in the truck," I point out, rubbing my temples, fighting off the tension headache threatening to bombard me and slow me down. I can't let that happen. "I mean, would a frantic parent stop off and pick up a friend to join them at the hospital? Besides," I add, "where is the nearest hospital to their home? Was he even traveling in that direction?"

"Good point." A quick search reveals that he was not, in fact, driving toward any of the three hospitals in the area. So much for that.

He takes it back to the beginning, starting again with the first piece of footage. "There must be a point where we can pick up what this person looks like."

"I could forward the footage over to the digital forensics team," I offer. "They might be able to sharpen the image."

"Yes, let's do that," he agrees. "Whoever it is,

they're the key to this. I feel it in my gut." He presses a closed fist to that particular location.

"I know what you mean," I concur, nodding slowly as my own gut urges me to pursue this lead.

"Who could it be?" he asks me. I'm sure it's mostly rhetorical, that he doesn't expect me to pull a name out of thin air. Considering the amount of information I've gathered, I'm sure he's hoping I can come up with a solid theory. So am I.

If only it were that easy. "I spoke with a colleague of his earlier," I explain. "And the general feeling around the office was that Ryan might've been having an affair. He's been very distracted, taking the same sort of calls he was getting at home. Always checking his phone, on edge, disappearing randomly and with no explanation."

"Could that be who we're looking at here?"

"It could be. Or … " I hate to think it, I really do, but the possibility exists. "It could be Ryan's affair partner is also married or at least seriously involved with someone else. My mind immediately jumped to the possibility of an affair when Jessica first described the phone call she overheard. Now … "

I turn my attention back to the screen and the person sitting in the passenger seat. "I wonder if we're looking at a betrayed husband or boyfriend in that seat. What if he found out and demanded Ryan go somewhere with him? That might've been who was calling the night Jessica overheard it, for all we know."

"The phone records should help clear that up," he points out.

"Yes, they should."

"But what about the baby? That doesn't explain why Ryan would take the baby."

Good point. I lace my fingers behind my head and blow out a frustrated sigh. "Well, leaving the baby behind would've meant waking Jessica up. If he were trying to hide something from her, he wouldn't want to explain why all of a sudden, he needed to go out so late at night. I can see him having to decide between bringing Isabel and spilling his guts to his wife."

"Bringing the baby probably seemed like the lesser of two evils."

"Exactly."

He scrubs a hand over his scruffy cheek. "He might also have thought whoever this person is, they wouldn't do anything rash with a baby involved."

"You're right," I agree. "That's a great point."

"This isn't my first rodeo," he reminds me. I'm almost embarrassed—I might've sounded patronizing when I said that—but he laughs it off. "All right. Now, we wait for the digital forensic team to find out if they can sharpen the image. In the meantime, we cross our fingers and hope the phone records are released sooner rather than later."

"I'll place a call to Special Agent Childs and explain the urgency. I'm sure he can get results for us a lot faster than either of us would be able to on our own." I leave him, speed walking to my office, already pulling up Childs' contact in my phone. He answers by the time I've reached my desk.

"Tell me you found something that quickly," he urges once he's picked up.

"As a matter of fact, I have," I tell him. "And I'm going to need you to move heaven and earth to get those phone records released so we know who Ryan has been talking to, because he was not alone with the baby that night. There was someone in the truck with him."

# 10

## Alexis

"Thank you so much for allowing me to come back."

Jessica shrugs, releasing a silent laugh. "What am I supposed to do? Say no? At this point, I'll do anything." Her arms fold across her stomach and a pained expression touches the corners of her eyes.

"When was the last time you slept?" I ask out of concern. It's probably not my place to ask a question like that, but the woman is suffering. The bags under her eyes are more pronounced, and it looks like she's lost weight in the handful of days since the disappearance. Dropping enough weight to make the difference noticeable leads me to suspect she's not taking care of herself at all.

"I sleep when I can." She shrugs, looking and sounding vague. "I don't know. I'm always afraid I'm going to miss something."

Immediately, my thoughts go to Ethan. "How is your son holding up?" I ask on our way through the house. It's considerably less neat than it was on Friday, only four days ago. Then again, some of that has to do with the number of bouquets and cards scattered on every flat surface. Entering the kitchen means stepping into a room filled with cookie trays, baskets of pastries, cakes sitting beneath glass domes. The neighborhood has come out in force—I wonder how the two of them are supposed to eat it all.

"He was determined to go to school today." There's a note of pride in her voice. "He is such a good boy. He wants so much to make things easier for me."

Just like me. At first, anyway. When weeks stretched into months, then into years, I eventually became too tired to carry that heavy burden. Making sure everyone was all right, being good, tiptoeing through my own life so as to not make waves. After all, everybody was already going through enough. I didn't want to add to it. But everybody has their breaking point.

Fretting over Ethan isn't going to help me find Ryan and Isabel. "Is it still all right for me to go through Ryan's home office, like we discussed?"

"Of course. I mean, I doubt he would like it very much if he knew, but circumstances being what they are and everything, I'm not going to say no." She leads the way down to the basement, which is as neat and orderly as I expected. There is a little clutter here and there—folders, tall cardboard tubes gathered together in the corners.

"His plans," Jessica explains while flipping on the lights. At the moment, there's a set of plans spread out across a long drafting table. He must've been in the middle of working on them, with half of the space still blank.

There's almost something ritualistic in the way I pull on my gloves, prepared to dig in and see what I can find. "I promise, I'll do my best not to disturb things too much."

"Whatever you have to do." I'm almost sorry when she settles on one of the steps leading up to the kitchen. Then again, how would I feel if there were a stranger in my home, going through my husband's things? I would probably be a little wary. Not to mention the way it must be torturing her, having no answers.

"Honestly," she says once I have begun sifting through the folders on the desk, "I'm not sure what you could find here. I tidy up down here sometimes, when he's in the middle of a really tight deadline, and I've never found anything strange or inexplicable."

She would say that, wouldn't she? "To be fair," I murmur, "you weren't looking for anything in particular."

"And you are?" She's not challenging me. It seems like she's genuinely interested, as well as concerned.

"Sort of."

"But why?" Her voice rises a step in pitch. "What have you found? What's changed?"

I'm not going to get anywhere if I'm bombarded by questions. "I explained before, when we first met, we can't afford to discount any possibility. That means finding out if there were people your husband dealt with who you didn't know about. That doesn't mean there was anything questionable happening. Only that there could be others with insight into your husband's dealings lately. That's all."

She's not convinced, probably because she's too intelligent to be so easily placated. But if she's that intelligent, how can she still blindly insist her husband wasn't up to anything? She must have seen something if his coworkers did. Or was she that distracted by the baby, and Ethan, and work, and everything else going on in her life?

One thing is for sure, the man is not as organized as he seems on the surface. Being tidy and being organized are two different things. Yes, he keeps things in neat piles, but what's in those piles is a complete hodgepodge. There's no system. Purchase orders are mixed up with memos, handwritten notes featuring, what I guess are, dimensions, measurements. Random receipts.

"Oh," Jessica explains when I find a slim, leather bound book at the bottom of the pile. "That's his day planner. He's a little old-fashioned when it comes to stuff like that—I always tease him about it. I mean, who doesn't schedule things on their phone or in Outlook?"

That's a good question. He's a very particular sort of person. I flip open the cover, scanning the contents. He has very neat handwriting—at least that much is working in my favor. I don't have to struggle over indecipherable chicken scratch.

Mark said Ryan has been acting strangely for

months. I decide to flip back to entries Ryan made starting in September and work my way forward. I can say one thing for him, he's disciplined when it comes to keeping an accurate record of his day-to-day life.

*Diner with X.* The entry grabs my attention. Who is X? Flipping ahead, I find half a dozen similar entries in October, November. I wonder if any of the receipts I've found so far lineup with these dates. But why would he keep a record of something he was clearly secretive about? Otherwise, why not use a name? The more I find out about this man, the more questions I'm left with. There is particular, and there's peculiar.

I'm about to flip back to September when something else catches my eye. Not the entry as much as the time of the appointment he made a note of. Without looking back at Jessica, I ask, "Does Ryan make a habit of scheduling meetings late at night?"

"I don't think so. I mean, I'm here. I would know."

Would she? Considering he sneaked out of the house with Isabel while she was sleeping, I have to wonder. Was this not the first time he's done something like that? Months ago, there was no baby to consider. He might have made a habit of ducking out while his wife slept. This time, he couldn't do it so easily.

One after another, I find cryptic entries at 11:00, 11:30. *BD. FL.* Who do those letters stand for? Or are they locations? What was he really into?

Before closing the book to continue looking around, instinct leaves me flipping ahead to the present—rather, the recent past. The night he went missing.

In the 10:30 slot, he jotted down the initials XXX.

It wasn't a random, spur-of-the-moment meet up. He had planned it, or someone else had. Suddenly, his compassion toward his wife—telling her to rest while he cared for Isabel—has taken on a different shape. He wanted Jessica asleep so he could get out unnoticed.

I slide the appointment book to one side, intending to take it into evidence, but accidentally knock a ruler onto the floor. Crouching to pick it up, I happen to glance at the wall the drafting table sits against. It's dark under there, of course, but not dark enough to conceal the outline of what could be a door.

My scalp is tingling as I stand. "Can you help me move this?" I ask, already taking one of the table's short ends in my hands. "I need to pull it away from the wall."

We slide it a few feet, until I have a clear view of what is obviously a hidden door embedded in the wall. "Did you know about this?" I ask, looking her way as I use my phone to take photos. I want to be sure to document this as accurately as possible.

"No." She sounds confused, overwhelmed. "I mean, now that I think about it, I might have noticed that door when we first moved in. But then Ryan put the table in front of it, and I never really thought about it again."

Convenient for him. Once I've documented its current state, I go down on one knee and press a hand against the wood panel. It springs open, swinging silently, revealing a safe.

Rather than ask Jessica if she knew about it, I look at her, watching her process this. "Why is that there?" she asks, chewing her thumbnail, her eyes wide. Do I believe her? I think I do. She seems genuinely baffled.

There is an electronic keypad on the door. What would he use as a combination? Jessica gives me everyone's birthdates, the date of their anniversary, but nothing works. After exhausting those options, I go back through the many notes and scraps of paper crammed into those folders. Maybe, just maybe, he kept it somewhere.

"Wait a second." Jessica makes a move like she's going to grab something, but my soft grunt makes her stop short.

"Sorry," I murmur, "but I have to make sure nothing is moved when it shouldn't be. Just to make sure nothing's been compromised."

She settles for pointing. "There used to be a sticky note here, on the corner of the table. It was bright yellow, and it had numbers on it. I never touched it. I figured it was just something he needed to remember"

I saw a yellow post it on the inside of one of those folders. I go through them rapidly, flipping one open after another, before finding the note on which Ryan wrote six numbers. When I enter those six numbers into the keypad, the door opens.

"Stand back, please," I urge, grabbing my phone so I can photograph whatever is inside.

Jessica gasps at the stacks of cash inside. "What?" she whispers. "Where ... How ... "

Good questions. It's not only the cash I'm interested in, but the presence of four cell phones, all of which I photograph before taking a ledger out and revealing endless line items documenting what have to be transactions. Five thousand, ten thousand, it goes on and on. There are larger amounts, too. Fifty, a hundred thousand. What do they represent? What was he really doing?

A glance at Jessica reveals a woman in deep distress, deeper than what she already struggled with. "I swear," she breathes, shaking her head. "I've never seen any of this before. Why would he have this?"

She looks at me, her chin quivering. "What was he doing? Why did he have all that money?"

I would like answers to those questions, too. One thing is abundantly clear by the time I begin bagging things up to take to the station; if Ryan McAllister was having an affair, it could very well have been the least of his problems.

## 11

## Alexis

By the time I'm finished attaching photocopies of Ryan's ledger entries and appointments to an enormous corkboard in one of the police station's conference rooms, I'm bleeding from several paper cuts and a little dizzy from the smell of printer toner. I'm pretty sure I used an entire ream of paper, or close to it.

Chief Myers lets out a heavy sigh, standing beside me with his arms folded as he takes it all in. "I think we can safely say this is bigger than we originally anticipated."

I have to chuckle at his understatement. "How are we doing on that footage we requested?" I ask. Before I effectively claimed the station copier for myself, I pinpointed several dates in Ryan's appointment book which featured locations where meetings would be taking place. Barbershop, hardware, florist, diner. Chief Myers contacted those businesses on my behalf while I made copies.

"We got a couple responses. I was coming in to tell you the files were sent over."

Rather than return to my office, I turn to my laptop, set up on the conference table along with receipts and handwritten notes. I pulled from Ryan's basement. The chief saved the files on the shared drive and I use my login credentials to access them.

"What was the date and time of the hardware store entry? I ask.

"Thursday, January eighteenth," he reports. "11:15."

My heart is pounding as I locate that date and time. What was he doing there? Who was he meeting? These questions rattle around in my brain until I witness a man matching Ryan's description enter the frame in the bottom right corner. The chief grunts softly but doesn't say a word, just as drilled-in as I am. What was he doing? Everything about the man's body language screams nerves—his hands are thrust into his coat pockets as he rocks back-and-forth on his heels. His head moves one way, then the other. He's looking for someone, waiting.

"I wish it was a clearer image," the chief whispers, and I agree, but the snow that was falling at the time makes it difficult to get a clear look at his face.

Suddenly, Ryan turns like he heard something behind him. That would mean he's facing the alley between the hardware store and the shop next to it. "Come on," I whisper, digging my nails into my palm, hoping against hope. "Show yourself."

Slowly, a dark figure emerges, and Ryan backs up a little. "Afraid of this guy?" Chief Myers asks. I would put money on it. Ryan's shoulders are hunched up around his ears, his chin tucked in close to his chest. He's protecting himself, whether he realizes it or not. But why? From what?

The best lead we come up with is the presence of a large watch on the man's left wrist when he pulls a hand from his coat pocket and points menacingly at Ryan. I pause the footage at the point where the watch is clearest, but it's still not much to go on. "I'll send this over to the forensics team for them to clean it up," I offer.

"And I'll have a couple of my deputies go through the rest of the footage to see if we can find this guy again, or anybody else Ryan was meeting with," the chief decides.

He then looks around at the pages spread out across the table. "This has all the marks of a drug ring," he observes. "Not that I want to lead us in one direction or another before we have more information, but that's what keeps coming to mind. Shady characters, late-night meetings, and some of these initials."

He turns back to the corkboard, scanning the copies before tapping a finger against a ledger entry. I blew it up a little to make it easier to read. "The initials. BD. FL."

"What do you think it means?"

"All I know is, there are two frequent drug-related offenders whose names came to mind as soon as I saw this. Bud Drake, Frankie Lewis. Mid-level guys, soldiers. Arrested on drug trafficking, but somehow their slimy lawyers always get them out on one technicality or another. They're what you'd call my white whale," he admits. "I can't pin them down."

"They show up a lot in the appointment book." I point out multiple entries featuring those initials. "Of course, we can't be sure these are the same people."

"Look at this." He cross references the January eighteenth appointment with a ledger entry dated the next day. "January nineteenth. Fifty-thousand."

Now, it's a matter of lining up each appointment with a corresponding entry. He's right. It looks like these meetings correspond to incoming cash or shipments. Either way, Ryan was in charge of keeping track of everything.

"Why?" I ask, studying the pattern. "He's not an accountant. I would expect somebody in that line of work to be in charge of tracking cash flow."

"That could be part of the reason why he's doing it. Who would suspect an architect? Like you said, this isn't his line of work, numbers and such. It would be a good cover. A respected professional, a family man who lives a quiet life."

"And it would explain all of the sudden, out-of-character disappearing acts he's been pulling at work," I venture. "I doubt he can tell these people to hold on if they're demanding something from him. He has to drop everything and move."

"That makes more sense than him running off in the middle of the day to meet up with a girlfriend."

"And that makes it easier to imagine him taking a risk like bundling up the baby and ducking out with her," I conclude. "These are not people who will accept excuses."

"Could be he got himself in deeper than he ever intended. This is a smart guy we're talking about," he points out, sinking into a chair in front of the corkboard and gazing up at it. "Smart people always think they can keep things under control. Other people might have gotten burned before, but not them."

"Pure hubris," I murmur, and he nods.

"Pride goes before the fall, like they say." He sighs and shakes his head like he's disappointed. "They never find out until it's too late that there's a reason organizations like this are able to stay in business, and it's not because they're so kind and understanding. They know exactly how to pull people in and hold them so they can't get away."

Nothing he's saying is news to me, but it sends a chill down my spine just the same. No wonder Ryan was acting strangely. They were probably putting pressure on him.

"It still doesn't explain how he fits into any of this." Chewing my lip, mulling it over, I ask, "Why would the numbers guy need to suddenly leave work in the middle of the day?"

"He might not only be the numbers guy. He might track the activities behind these transactions. Incoming shipments and such." He shrugs when I turn his way. "Like we said. The least likely suspect."

I have to remind myself once again this is all speculation. We don't have any solid proof.

But my gut knows when it hears something plausible. No matter how many times I tell myself to be fair and balanced, there's no denying how plausible all of this sounds. Everything fits together in a bigger, grimmer picture.

## 12

## Alexis

The good, warm weather seems to be holding. I can almost believe winter is over, though having spent my formative years in this area, I know better than to let my guard down. I'm cautiously optimistic, though, as I park the Corolla just beyond the tall, wrought iron gate leading into the cemetery. With so many of my thoughts lately having to do with Maddie, it only feels right to pay her a visit. She's been alone out here for so long.

There's a big difference from my most recent visit. No fresh crust of snow on the ground, no gray skies. The air is heavy with the scents of life waking back up, of rich earth and the promise of what's to come.

In some ways, it feels almost perverse to be thinking along those lines while visiting a grave. To be imagining new life springing up. I've been spending too much time locked in my own head, that much is obvious by the time Maddie's headstone comes into view. The fact that it sits untouched lessens the tension

I didn't realize had locked my shoulders and back in knots. Tyler isn't here. He's miles away, spilling his guts, hoping for a plea deal somewhere down the line. He can't leave any creepy notes or flowers now.

Only I am here, touching my hand to the cold stone bearing my sister's name. "Hey," I whisper, running my hand along the smooth granite. "It's me. I've been thinking a lot about you lately. I hope you don't mind me stopping by unannounced."

It's silly, talking to her that way, but it makes me feel closer to her, too. It's not like anybody can hear me—I turn a slow circle, scanning the entire field around me, and I see no one. I guess it's busier around here on weekends, holidays. The middle of a weekday afternoon isn't exactly prime time for a trip to the cemetery.

"This is the second time I'm visiting you in a month." Bending down, I clear leaves away from the base of my sister's headstone before leaving at its base a bouquet of cheerful daisies. "But when you think about it, considering I never visited before the last time, my average is still extremely low."

It's so peaceful out here. Quiet. I can gather my thoughts as I take a seat on the ground, resting cross legged on a patch of fresh grass. "Well, there's one good thing," I announce. "I'm not going to find any surprises waiting for me anymore. We got him."

Why is there no joy in my heart? I've imagined this moment, announcing to my sister I had caught the man who killed her. Before Russell Duffy was captured, that was my childish fantasy. And for years, I tried to tell myself I could rest knowing her killer was facing justice.

Until I came back to town and found out how wrong I was. How wrong we all were. "I haven't talked to dad yet about having Russell exonerated," I murmur, staring off into the woods behind the cemetery. I check in with myself, listening to my instincts, but they're silent this time around. There's no sense of anybody watching from out there. "I know I'll have to eventually bring it up, especially since the team that's trying to help him wants me to participate. It will mean having to see Tyler again," I remind myself, "but I always knew that was bound to happen. That I would have to look him in the eye again."

"And I want to," I add with determination in my voice. "I plan to be there when he is sentenced. Even if it isn't for what he did to you, Maddie, so long as I can see him put away for the rest of his life."

I cast a guilty look toward the headstone bearing the dates marking the beginning and the end of my sister's life. Only fifteen years. She's been gone longer than she was here. It doesn't feel possible, but the math doesn't lie.

"I can't believe you've been gone for so long. There are times it feels like just yesterday. When I have a nightmare and I'm thrown right back. It all feels so fresh and real and immediate. I don't know if there's ever going to be a day when it doesn't feel like that."

I have to take a breath and swallow back the worst of the pain tightening my throat. "But can I tell you a secret?" I ask, echoing the words we so often used when she was alive. When I had a big sister. "Sometimes, I think it's better this way. Otherwise, I might start to forget, and I don't want to forget you. But then I hate all of my memories of you being wrapped up in the ugliness of what he did to you. You would think after twenty years and a doctorate degree, I would have all of this figured out."

A soft breeze touches my skin, pushing my hair back from my forehead. When I close my eyes, I can almost imagine it's my big sister's hand sweeping my overgrown bangs out of my eyes, the way she used to do sometimes as she passed by. When she would find me reading on the porch, on her way out to see another friend. She had so many.

"Mom and Dad are doing well," I tell her. "I mean, you might already know that. I'm not sure how all of this works and how much you can see. They're learning to live together again. They're different people now," I muse, twirling the stem of a dead leaf between my fingers.

I wanted to visit them today, but they were out when I made my impulsive visit to the house. A text from Mom revealed they had gone antiquing. My parents, going antiquing the way they used to so long ago. When they first wanted to renovate the house and turn it into a bed and breakfast. "I think they're really going to go ahead with it," I announce with a smile. "I walked out to the garage, where Dad had his workshop, and it smelled like sawdust. Just like it used to."

My eyes fill with tears and I choke out, "Oh, Maddie, I can't tell you what that meant. It's like they're both coming back to life. Maybe they needed each other before they could start."

The sunshine feels good against my skin. I lean on my elbows, tipping my head back and closing my eyes. "I wish you could've met Mitch," I confess with a sigh. "You would've liked him so much. I swear, there are times when it feels like he's not real, like I dreamed him up in my head. Somebody who sees me, all of me, and still wants to be with me. I almost feel sorry for the poor guy," I admit, chuckling.

A rush of cool air rolls past me, and my heart aches. I would swear I can hear her laughter carried on that breeze, picked up in the flapping of wings as birds leave the trees. "You thought I was a pest when we were kids? I can be a lot worse now," I admit, laughing softly. "But he doesn't mind, somehow. I keep waiting for the time when he'll decide I'm not worth the trouble, but it hasn't happened yet. I don't want it to ever happen, of course, but I'm afraid it will. What if he decides I'm too much trouble? What do I do then? But then, what if he doesn't? What do I do if that happens?" I have to force a deep breath when my thoughts start spiraling.

"Gosh, I wish you were here," I tell her again once I'm calmer. "I mean, you know Mom. The second I mention something like this, she's going to start planning a wedding. She probably already has," I add with a chuckle. "Even when we were kids together, you were always so level headed. I have to believe you would still be level headed now. And I could go to you, my big sister, to ask for advice. You wouldn't be jonesing for a new baby in the family the way Mom would—though who knows?" I point out. "You might have been salivating for a niece or nephew. I guess I'll never know, will I?"

At the end of the day, that's what hurts the most. I'll never know what might have been. Maddie's life will always be a question mark in the middle of a very short chapter that was never completed.

"It's been really hard lately for me to put a sense of distance between myself and the cases I'm working on. Right now, for instance," I explain, "the man who is missing has a little boy who is a couple of years younger than I was when you left us. I know I have to stop comparing us, but I can't help it sometimes. I look at him, and all I see is the confusion I felt. And then I remember everything that came after, and my heart aches for him. Mitch is always reminding me I can't help everybody, I can't solve the world's problems. And of course, I know that up here."

I tap two fingers to the side of my head. "But in here?" My hand drifts down to my chest, resting over my heart. "It's a different story. And on some level, only I will ever understand that. As patient as he is, as much as he tries to relate, there are some things you don't know until you go through them."

My sigh is swallowed by the soft breeze before I sink into silence, gazing up at the blue sky and the trees that have stood silent sentry over my sister's grave.

## 13

## Alexis

Mitch would hate it if he knew I was doing this. Even I hate it but I know there's no choice. If I'm going to learn more about the criminal underworld around here, I need to spend time in the sort of establishment where these people hang out, exchange information, that sort of thing. Speculation is useless, a waste of time without facts to hang it on.

Which is why I'm here, parked half a block down from a rough looking bar which intel sources confirm is something of a hangout for low-level criminals in the area. They are hardly the best of the best, these people. Petty criminals, fairly low stakes for the most part. What I am more interested in learning about tonight is about the networks around here. Who knows who. Who does what. It's like a spiderweb, these connections, or maybe like a ball of yarn after a cat has gotten into it. A mass of tangles I now need to work out.

That's what gets me out of the car, my attention

pointed toward the rusted screen door which bangs jarringly every time someone walks in or out. A corner bar, like so many others, with neon signs in the window advertising the brands of beer sold inside. Sometimes the door opens in time for a burst of raucous laughter to flow out into the chilly night. A man in a fleece lined jacket that's seen better days stumbles out, rights himself, then begins the process of navigating the sidewalk. It's not even very late at night, but he's staggering like he's spent hours on a barstool. At least he doesn't try to get behind the wheel of a car —I'm not sure I could stand back and watch that happen, even if I'm not exactly advertising the fact that I'm law enforcement. Tonight, I'm a civilian, and I'm glad I chose an old pair of jeans and scuffed up sneakers. I don't want to stand out. If this is truly somewhere for the criminal element to gather, they'll be savvy enough to spot me at a hundred paces.

Stepping inside means immediately being smacked in the face by the smell of beer, plus the stench of stale cigarette smoke. It doesn't seem like anyone is actively smoking in here – no doubt the odor sank into the ceiling tiles over decades of customers chain smoking, the sort of thing that doesn't go away on its own. The light is dim, the lamps hanging over tables lining the far wall barely giving off enough of a glow for people at the same table to see each other clearly. A TV mounted in the corner plays a boxing match, and a handful of patrons seem very interested in the outcome. Maybe they have money riding on it.

Settling down at the bar, I ask the thick-necked

bartender for a lager. I thought about how to approach this the entire way here, going through possible lines of questioning. How do I express interest while seeming innocent?

When the bartender slides a pint glass my way, I offer a grin. "Thanks. I was hoping to meet somebody here tonight, but I don't see him around. Did he maybe show up, then leave? I am running a little late."

"Can't say. Describe him for me," he suggests, rinsing glasses at the same time. His ease with multitasking and his comfort and efficiency behind the bar tell me he has probably worked here a long time and has seen plenty of things. The faint suspicion in his voice makes me wonder how many women have come in here looking for a boyfriend or a husband who isn't supposed to be out and about.

I describe Ryan based on the photos I've seen. "He's pretty straight edge," I add with a laugh, glancing toward the gathering of fierce looking men absorbed in the boxing match. "Like, you would expect to see him behind a computer, know what I mean?"

"Does he wear a wedding ring?" he asks, narrowing his eyes.

"We're just friends," I assure him with a smile. "But yes, he is married. He's … " Shifting my gaze to the right, then the left, I lean across the bar ever so slightly. "He was dealing with some deliveries for a mutual friend. I was supposed to give him some info, but he's not here."

"Deliveries?" He exchanges a look with a man

sitting several stools down from where I am. In the reflection in the mirror running behind the bar, I find a middle-aged bruiser with a bald head and a scar running above his left eye. Now he's paying attention, angling his body toward me.

"What's this guy's name who you're looking for?" he asks in a voice that brings to mind rocks running through a tumbler. One of his ham-sized fists is curled around a pint glass that looks like a toy in comparison.

"Ryan," I whisper. "You know him? I really need to see him."

"Hasn't been around in a while. But yeah, he was here, what?" He looks at the bartender, who shrugs. "Sometimes two or three times a week. But it's been days since he and Viper met up here, right?"

"Yeah, that's about right," the bartender agrees. "They always take the corner booth. Haven't seen Viper, either," he adds. "Hadn't thought about it until now."

Viper. Why not hang a sign around his neck saying *I'm a criminal?* Thinking fast, I ask, "Does Viper wear a big, shiny watch?" I ask, pointing to my wrist. "And a long, black coat?"

"Yeah, and he's usually wearing that knit hat," the bartender confirms. "I don't ever see him without it on. Couldn't tell you his hair color, come to think of it."

"He's got sorta reddish hair," the bald man says. "I think. But it could be brown. Skinny."

"You think?" The bartender shakes his head. "Last time I saw him, I remember thinking it looked like he put some weight on. But he could've been layered up, with the cold outside and all."

The bald man shrugs. "Wish we could help you, but both of them have been MIA."

"Do you know where Viper might hang out?" It's a long shot, and that's an understatement, but I have to try.

The men exchange a brief smirk. "Let's just say probably no place you'd want to visit," the bartender assures me with a laugh before pouring a pair of beers for other customers. "I mean, you could try, but I wouldn't if I were you."

So everybody knows this Viper guy is bad news. Why was Ryan meeting him here? It's miles away from the house and probably no place anyone would think to look for him, but what in the world was he into? How does somebody who by all accounts was a successful architect, an honest man, get wrapped up in something like this? Do they have a recruiting program? It doesn't make any sense.

I slide a few bills across the bar and take a couple sips of my beer before thanking the men and making my escape. Instead of lingering in my parking space, I pull away from the bar and drive a few blocks, watching to be sure I'm not followed. It didn't seem like I aroused any suspicions back there, but there's no way of knowing for sure.

Once it looks like I'm alone, I pull into the first available parking spot in front of a shuttered convenience store and pull out my phone to call the chief for info. "Viper? The name does sound familiar," he tells me. "I feel like we've come across this guy before."

"Can you please do me a favor? Check your records and see if there are any known hangouts for this guy." As I speak, my head is on a swivel, eyeing the shadows. Something about this area and the time of night has my instincts on high alert.

"Don't tell me you plan on going out tonight looking for him."

"I'm already in the area," I remind him, busy pulling up notes I took after combing through Ryan's planner and ledger. "And there are a few locations here, the ones we managed to track down from his appointment entries. Maybe there is some overlap we can look into."

"You should have backup with you."

"Negative," I reply, ignoring his heavy sigh. "I'm not going to show myself. I would like to take a look, is all, from the safety of my car." I mean, I know I take too many risks, but I'm not deluded.

After another fifteen minutes or so of cross-refer-encing locations and descriptions, I plug into the GPS an address that's shown up more than once in Ryan's personal effects. Not for the first time do I silently thank my lucky stars for the team working behind the scenes to make sense of a bunch of scribbled, poorly coded entries. I don't know if I would have time to do all of that and chase down leads the way I'm doing now, driving to a warehouse in an industrial area posi-tioned only a mile or two away from a major shipping hub.

From where I park, I can see the lights out there, glowing like a beacon. Trucks pull in and out at all times, delivering packages, picking up shipments to be transported elsewhere.

"This location was originally part of the hub," Chief Parkins explains over the phone as I watch the smaller, remote building. It's not easy to make out much of it in the darkness, but from where I sit, it's obvious the place isn't used for anything legitimate nowadays. The parking lot is completely overgrown, with weeds growing thick, and tall from cracks in the asphalt. Vines creep up along the façade, almost completely covering the cinderblock in some cases. Using binoculars, I observe the handful of people wandering in and out. A few of them smoke, a couple of them type on their phones. This is not a social gathering, though.

"I'm going to take some photos," I announce, using my camera phone to snap them. The handful of lights near the warehouse entrance are enough to illuminate the men, even if the images are slightly grainy thanks to the way I have to zoom in. Still, they're sharp enough to make out details of faces and even a few tattoos. "I'm sending them to the field office. I'm pretty sure I recognize one or two of them based on identifying marks—one of them has a neck tattoo I've seen in mugshots, for sure. I should have some concrete details by morning."

With that, it's time to go. I don't trust myself making the drive back to Broken Hill much later than this, when my eyes are already tired. Then there's the thought of Mitch waiting for me. I can't imagine a time when I won't look forward to getting home to him.

For now, it's enough that I'm confident I'm getting closer all the time.

Even if part of me can't help wanting to burn the midnight oil. Sometimes, it's just as important to take a step back. I have to keep that at the front of my mind as I pull away, leaving heaven only knows what behind me.

# 14

## Alexis

"I have to say, doing inventory is a lot more pleasant with you around." Mitch grins my way from behind a stack of boxes. "Less creepy, too."

Narrowing my eyes, I retort, "Wow. When you set out to compliment a girl, you really know how to make her feel special."

"What can I say? It gets a little creepy around here in the evening, after I've closed the store." He looks around the space on the second floor of the building, where the store's stock is kept. There's also a pair of recliners up here, a TV, and a twin bed in the back corner of the room.

Eyeing the bed, I ask, "But you managed to sleep up here? Even when you were creeped out?"

He chuckles, shrugging before going back to the spreadsheet on his tablet. "What can I say? I spent many nights burning the midnight oil down in the kitchen, perfecting my recipes. Sometimes I needed to duck up here and get a few hours' sleep if I wanted to get any sleep at all before opening for the day."

It's funny. We are so similar in so many ways—which is probably what brought us together in the first place when we were kids. That same drive and determination that often makes him grind his teeth when I'm the subject is exactly what made it possible for him to build his business. Granted, there's a difference between working twenty hours at a stretch in a bookstore café and chasing kidnappers through blizzards, but still.

He frowns at the arrangement of boxes I'm currently using as a table, digging through files, cross referencing names on my laptop. "So much for cataloging what's in those," he sighs, nodding toward my makeshift workstation.

I look down at it, then up at him. "I'm sorry. I just need to—"

"I know." He chuckles while making a note on the tablet. "And I'm only kidding. I would still rather have you here than not."

There is a definite swelling in my chest, almost like my heart is expanding. He wants me around. There are still times I wonder why he wants to have anything to do with me, as scattered as I can be. As distant as things have gotten in the recent past. I guess rather than question my incredible good luck, I should thank my lucky stars and work on being the girlfriend he needs. Which means working here, with him, rather than doing this at home.

Not that I mind. Like he said I'd rather be with him than alone.

He glances toward my screen in passing. "What are you looking at?"

"I'm trying to connect a few of the names of people I saw last night," I explain. "Cross referencing known activities, known associates. There has to be something tying them all together. Something I can use to direct me to whoever sits at the top of this pyramid or whatever it is."

"Well, I can tell you one thing." His hands close over my shoulders from behind. "I would much rather see you doing legwork like this in a safe environment."

I touch my cheek to the back of one hand before returning to the work in front of me. It seems like every rock I overturn leaves a half dozen slimy creatures crawling out from underneath. Not a bad metaphor, considering the nature of the men I'm researching. If anything comes to mind when I imagine them, it's slimy things. Creatures that make their homes in dark places, hoping no one will see. Eventually, I'm going to overturn the right rock. It's only a matter of time.

Time which I don't have. There is still no sign of Ryan or Isabel and while the connection to the local underworld is a huge break, that's the last big break we've gotten in two days. How does he fit into this? What has he been doing all this time? And why wouldn't they at least drop the baby off someplace? I can't get that question out of my head. It's always running through the back of my mind no matter what I'm doing. Whatever Ryan did, Isabel is innocent.

Would these people be beyond selling a baby, considering everything else they do? I shudder at the thought but it makes me work harder. Is there any connection there? A line I can draw between the people I suspect Ryan has been involved with and a human trafficking ring? Am I wasting time by pursuing what could be a baseless theory?

"Hungry?"

My head snaps up suddenly enough to make Mitch fall back a step. "Sorry," he offers while holding out a plate of quiche, along with a pair of oversized chocolate chip cookies. "I had a feeling you were too deeply engrossed to listen to your stomach."

Right on cue, the stomach in question rumbles. It could be the aroma of the quiche, though, which I eagerly accept before cutting off a bite with my fork. How long was he downstairs without me realizing it? "You are an angel," I manage around a mouthful of flaky pastry and rich, cheesy egg.

"My halo goes a little crooked from time to time, but I'll take the compliment." He drops into the other armchair, glancing over the legal pad in front of me. "Viper. Who's that?"

The word is scrawled at the top of the page, and as I've sat and turned a hundred questions over in my head, I've darkened the letters while doodling absent-mindedly. Now they jump out against the yellow page. "That's the question," I admit.

"Not exactly the most imaginative nickname."

"Something tells me these guys aren't in this business because they have robust imaginations," I point out. "If they did, they might find a way to make a legitimate living that doesn't involve sneaking around at night and hurting people."

"You know, that is something I've wondered about more than once." When I raise an eyebrow, he lifts his shoulder. "You know. Stories about these mastermind criminals. Guys who run these multi-million dollar empires based on doing everything they can to steal and cheat people and get around the law. How much good could they do, using all those smarts on something worthwhile?"

It's exactly the sort of question he would come up with, as decent and good as he is. "Not everybody is like you," I point out. Talk about the understatement of the century. "Not everybody is willing to work hard, the way you have."

"The way we both have," he reminds me.

I'm working hard now, and where is it getting me? "If only I knew where to find this guy, or even what he looks like."

"I thought you said those guys at the bar described him?"

"Yes, but it would've been nice if they were able to agree on a description. I don't know if this guy has red or brown hair or any hair at all. I guess it's not beyond the realm of possibility that he would have to change his appearance sometimes, but wouldn't it make more sense just to meet at a different location rather than always going to the same place?"

"Who knows?" There's faint laughter in Mitch's voice by the time he finishes his slab of quiche and sets the plate aside. "Maybe he does it for the fun of it."

"Oh, come on," I groan, laughing softly.

"Think about it. If I want to change things up around here? I can rearrange shelves, change the window display, change the seasonal decor. I can mix up the menu in the café, add new drink combinations for people who like their fancy coffee. What does this guy get to do to mix things up? Buy a new gun?"

Something about the way he says it makes me laugh. I feel like I shouldn't, like this is much too serious a topic to burst out laughing over, but it feels good. Like maybe it's how I'm supposed to feel right now. Like life doesn't have to be dark all the time.

"I'm trying to think of the last time I mixed things up," I admit, setting the work aside along with my plate.

"You should work on that."

"I should. I need a little more fun in my life," I announce before laughing at myself. "What a monumental decision. Alert the press, take out ads in the local paper."

"I'm not going to disagree with you." Mitch eyes me, one eyebrow arched. "Any thought as to what you might want to do?"

"Nothing specific. Just in general." My neck is stiff after sitting like this for so long, frozen in the same position. Rolling my head from side to side and massaging my tired muscles doesn't help all that much.

"Come here. Let me help." He pulls me to my

feet, and soon his large, capable hands go to work. Little by little, the ache melts away, until I have no choice but to lean against him with my cheek to his chest while he continues draining the tension from my body.

"You are much too good at this," I mumble against his soft sweater.

"I'm good at a lot of things."

I'm no fool. I hear the way his voice changed, the wry humor in it. The suggestive grin that tugs the corners of my mouth upward. "Like what?" Lifting my head, I look up at him. The wicked light in his eyes warms me all over.

"I'd be happy to show you." First, he kisses me while backing us up until we're standing next to the twin bed. "But we might need to lie down first."

"The bed's a little small, but I think I can make the sacrifice," I whisper before he kisses me again.

## 15

## Alexis

"Chief? You wanted to see me?" Standing in the doorway to his office, I hold up the sticky note I found on my desk a minute ago. Nothing like a bright yellow note filled with hastily scrawled words to make a girl's heart beat faster first thing in the morning.

"We got word from one of our informants." The man's eyes are practically gleaming. "He's been a bad boy lately and knows he better talk if he doesn't want to spend a good, long time in a cell."

"Who is this guy?" Mentally crossing my fingers, I accept the folder Chief Perkins holds out to me. While I flip through it, he explains what's inside.

"Larry Townsend. Thirty-four, could easily pass for fifty after all of his hard living. Knows he'd never make it a minute behind bars after all the intel he's given up over the years, but he can't seem to stay away from danger, either. He's been in and out of trouble since he was thirteen, this guy. Some people can't be helped."

There are a series of mugshots here depicting Larry's life through the decades. The last couple of photos reveal a man with hard, cold eyes and a permanently flattened nose. I wonder how many times it's been broken.

"Do you have a history with this guy?" I ask, flipping through his reports.

"He's been feeding us info for five, six years?" he muses, rubbing his temples. "He's never steered us wrong. I spoke to him personally when we brought him in last night after he was pulled over for reckless driving with a few thousand bucks worth of product in the car."

I release a soft whistle. "You'd think somebody would drive especially carefully at a time like that."

Smirking, he asks, "You would, wouldn't you? He's got a lot of connections in the local trade and claims he can provide information on the people Ryan appears to have been working with."

"When do we talk to him?" I'm champing at the bit as it is. As far as I'm concerned, we could have gone through this information on the way down to an interrogation room. The sooner I talk to the guy, the better.

"We are not going to talk to him," he replies. "You are."

"Me? You want me to go in alone?"

"That's what he wants," he explains. "He said he has plenty of information, but he wants to talk to the FBI."

"And do we normally let known offenders dictate terms like this?"

His brows draw together and I know I said too much, but I think it's a fair question. "When it's a matter of locating two missing people and possibly unraveling a much bigger operation than we first imagined?" he counters in a sharper voice than he's used with me so far.

"I didn't mean to be offensive." With my hands raised in front of me, I wince. "I'm sorry."

"Yeah, well, maybe I'm a little touchy." He scrubs a hand over his head before running it down the side of his face. It doesn't look like he's shaved in two or three days. "It's one thing, fighting these people when they're so darn good at hiding and deception. Then, somebody comes in from outside the department and helps uncover something this big? Bigger than we ever have? It's not easy to swallow."

I can understand that. This isn't the first time local law enforcement has been rubbed the wrong way by my presence. "We need to do everything we can to get that baby back safely," I remind him—and myself. "If it means speaking one-on-one with an informant, I can handle it. Let's set it up."

⌗

The chief was right about Larry passing for a man almost twenty years older. His weathered face and hard, dark eyes describe a life lived on the edge. In extremes.

Those eyes sweep the room frantically as he approaches the table where I wait. The diner sits more than a half hour outside town in an area so remote, I doubt anyone but drivers looking to avoid a clogged interstate ever venture past. In other words, it's perfect for our secret meeting.

"Larry?" I ask once he reaches me. This is definitely the man from the mugshots who used to be a pretty cute kid.

His head bobs sharply before he slides his tall, thin body into the padded booth. A waitress approaches and he orders coffee, while I ask for a grilled cheese sandwich. Mitch would be proud, knowing I've given a little thought to whether I'll eat today. "Thank you for coming out here," I murmur once we're on our own. Aside from a pair of potbellied, white-haired men reading newspapers at the counter, the diner is empty.

"I can't stay long. If anybody saw us together … " He taps his blunt fingertips against the table in a choppy rhythm.

"Sure. No problem." His coffee arrives, and I watch as he adds more sugar than anyone should drink at one time before he gulps half of it back all at once. "So, I understand you're familiar with the inner workings of the local trade."

He nods before sipping from the mug. "Yeah, that's right."

"And you might know something about the inner workings as they connect to a missing persons case currently under investigation?"

To my surprise, he snickers. "Can we talk like normal people? Yeah, I know stuff. A lot of stuff."

"About Viper?"

A jolt runs through him and makes the coffee cup tremble. It's a good thing it wasn't full. "Can we not use names out loud like that?"

He's terrified of this guy. "We're safe here."

"I'm glad you think so." After emptying the mug, he immediately looks around for the waitress. Is it the coffee or the sugar he needs more?

"What can you tell me about him?" I whisper. "I need to know how to find this guy. There's a good chance he's the key to unlocking this case."

"You don't get it." His eyes dart around and his fingers tap the table harder, faster. It's unnerving. "I'm telling you, this is dangerous."

We fall silent once my sandwich arrives, along with fresh coffee for him. "I have no doubt about that," I reply around a mouthful of melted cheese.

"Listen to me." His voice is like the crack of a whip —or a gunshot. It snaps my eyes open wider than before. "You pursue this, you're in for a world of trouble. Like, much worse than it is now. People like this guy, they feel threatened, and it's all over. You get what I'm saying?"

It isn't the words he uses, but rather the way he delivers them. The intensity simmering under the surface. He has to make me understand, or else. "Of course I do."

His thin lip curls upward in a sneer that chills me to the bone. "You think you do. You, like, do your training and you carry a badge and maybe you, like, work on cases. You think that means you understand people like them."

"I'm interested in your choice of words. People like them. What does that mean?" I ask.

"They're insane." The way he says it. Point-blank, deadpan, entirely serious. "Some people, they go through bad stuff in their life, and it sort of shuts them down inside. They have to, I don't know, let go of everything that made them human. It's like they forget feelings so they don't get caught up in them when they have to … you know."

He gazes out the window, pensive, scanning the roadway. "Kill people. And they can't let themselves think about the stuff they're shipping and selling and what it does to people, either. As far as they're concerned, that's not their problem."

A knowing smile twists his lips before his eyes meet mine again. "It's not like they're forcing anybody to buy it and use it, right? That's what they tell themselves."

He falls back against the vinyl padding behind him. "And then there's people who were born different. Wrong. Like they never had feelings in the first place. The work isn't what turned them into what they are. They do the work because it fits who they already were."

I can't help remembering what Mitch said last night about criminals who could've used their smarts in another way. This guy could've been something if he ever had the chance. His insight is breathtaking. "You're saying this Viper is that sort of person?"

"What I'm saying is, if an animal is cornered or feels threatened, it's going on the offensive to save itself. That's all it knows to do, right? There's no, like, reasoning or anything like that." He takes a pause, then adds, "Kill or be killed."

"I understand. I do." Taking another bite for the sake of appearances, I chew slowly while absorbing his message. While he hasn't answered any questions, per se, he's been valuable just the same. I understand the mentality of a man we know Ryan spent time with.

The sort of man who wouldn't have any problem discarding a baby?

"Okay." Opening my phone's voice memo app, I start a new recording. "Larry, I want you to tell me everything you know about Viper and his business."

His thin shoulders sink like he's disappointed, but he begins anyway.

# 16

# Alexis

"You need to be careful with this." Special Agent Childs' warning sets my teeth on edge, but I manage to hold back a groan of irritation—or disappointment in him. It could be a little bit of both.

Lowering my binoculars means I can't get a clear view of the activity taking place at the warehouse, but at the moment I'm a little more concerned with the note of apprehension in my boss's voice. "With all due respect, what is with the sudden interest in safety?"

"I always care whether my people are safe."

"Yes, but this is the third time you've urged me to be safe since you reviewed the recording of the interview. Why is that?"

"Because of the warning this Larry guy gave you." He pauses for effect before reminding me of what has been going through my mind on a constant loop ever since the meeting at the diner earlier today. Out of all of the information he provided, it was his final warning that seared itself onto my brain like a permanent brand. *"There will be more of these missing persons cases if you're not careful. Make sure you know what you're doing and you're ready to commit, because like I said, it's kill or be killed for him."*

Was that supposed to frighten me off? If anything, I'm more determined than ever to get my hands on this man. At the end of the day, that's all he is. Just a man. Not some ghost or some demon, but flesh and blood.

"We know how to handle people like this. Viper isn't unique. Maybe to a man like Larry, whose frame of reference isn't exactly broad." Using my binoculars again, I watch a large cargo truck pull away from the shipping hub a couple of miles down the road. Larry's information confirmed for me that this warehouse is a center of operations for the group. He heavily hinted at various shipments of narcotics and other contraband passing through the legitimate hub, while employees look the other way for a heavy fee. Those trucks are then diverted to this warehouse, where product is loaded and unloaded under cover of darkness.

"He said there should be another shipment through tomorrow. Midnight." Observing from a distance, I add, "All I need is my team in place."

"They're on their way down as we speak," he confirms. "I'll have them rendezvous with you at the local precinct."

In the meantime, then, I record footage. Men walking in and out, a couple of cars pulling away.

Nothing very interesting, nothing that points to something with teeth. Something I can use.

But there is a shipment coming in tomorrow, which is sure to translate into a goldmine of evidence. We have already used drone surveillance to determine a handful of places where other team members can lie in wait and observe from a different vantage point.

I need every piece of evidence we can put together. Every photo, video, not to mention anything we manage to gather after we perform our inevitable raid. Rather than going tomorrow, we'll wait another day– Viper and his friends will be especially guarded tomorrow, on high alert. It's better to hang back and watch them work before going in for the kill.

By the time I make it to the police station, there are a handful of cars in the visitors spots. Eight agents are already gathered in the conference room, going over my corkboard and the information spread across the conference table. They're all eager, bright eyed, sharp-jawed. Ready for action.

After introductions, I jump into running down the specifics as they currently stand before dividing the team into four pairs. After that, breaking up surveillance shifts is easy, and soon I'm sending the first team out to watch the warehouse while the others leave to settle in at their hotel for the night.

It doesn't feel right, going home. Have to remind myself that everything is in capable hands. I don't need to be present every second.

Even if I doubt I'll get much sleep.

"Here we go." I can hardly breathe from my position inside the unmarked car. A pair of long, unmarked trucks roll through the gate once the chain link slides open. In all of the time I've spent watching this location, not to mention the more than twenty-four hours split up among the team, no vehicles have rolled in this direction.

There's silence over my earpiece as we all hold our breaths and watch. It's exactly the way Larry described it. Trucks use the legitimate shipping hub as their destination, but are never processed. It makes me wonder how many people are on the drug ring's payroll. Is it worth it, I wonder? Maybe they don't like to think about it.

"Keep an eye out for that watch," I remind the others. "There's a good chance Viper will be here for this." I want a visual. I need a visual. Something to tie all of this to Ryan.

I lost track of the number of times I told Mitch there's nothing dangerous about what I'm doing tonight. That we would be so far from the warehouse, there wouldn't be a chance of us being spotted. I believe that, too.

Tomorrow is another story. "You have been through too many tense situations lately," Mitch reminded me when I broke the news to him. I didn't want to—the last thing he needs is to worry about me more than he already does. But if I got hurt, I would have to look him in the eye afterward and explain why he only learned I was performing a raid after the fact.

All things considered, I would rather err on the side of caution.

By now, Ethan might have given up hope on his dad ever coming home. It only took a few days before I started wondering if Maddie would ever come back to us. Sure, I was only ten, but Mom used to love watching TV shows about detectives and their cases. The one thing they always used to say was how crucial the first seventy-two hours were.

Once three days passed, I started to lose hope, even if I would never have admitted it out loud. I wanted to believe. I just … couldn't after a little while.

No kid deserves to have all of their illusions shattered at once. In Ethan's eyes, his dad is the greatest guy in the world. A kid at his age trusts their parents, believes they know what's right. That they're the good guys. That they don't do business with evil men.

"Agent Forrest?" one of the team murmurs. "Do you copy?"

"No, repeat." This isn't the time for me to get lost in memories and imaginings. There's too much riding on it—including my professional reputation, which I would rather not destroy by turning into a complete space cadet.

"I think we have our guy on the building's north side. Sending images." Only a few moments pass before the images in question fill the tablet mounted to my dashboard. I flip through them one at a time, a sense of certainty growing in my chest. Now I wish we were going in tonight. Having him there, so close, is almost too tempting to resist.

"Looks like our guy," I confirm. "I want eyes on him." The man with the watch and long coat wears an expression that makes me uneasy. I can't put my finger on why, exactly—he doesn't look angry or threatening the way Larry described him. Then again, maybe that's what's so unsettling. He's blank. He might as well be a mannequin, albeit a very tall, imposing mannequin. He's even wearing a knit hat, black like his coat. The way he was described to me.

More images come through, then more after that. Crates being unloaded, wheeled into the warehouse in stacks. Armed men stand on the loading dock. The first truck leaves surprisingly soon after its arrival—by now, they have this operation down to a science. The truck will now be loaded with its legitimate cargo back at the hub while the second truck is unloaded.

"I've counted nine different individuals," another one of the team members reports. "Though there are shadows visible through the windows, so there must be more inside."

"Keep count of individuals," I tell him. "On an average night, there might be half a dozen men around. Let's plan for at least twice that many, just in case." Because it won't be a shipment night, but there might still be merchandise in there. Larry was a little unclear as to just how swiftly product gets moved back out from the warehouse, but we might learn more about that between now and tomorrow depending on the flow of traffic in and out of here.

It's past two in the morning by the time I leave my vantage point while the others go back to their shifts. I'm due in Chief Perkins' office at eight o'clock tomorrow morning and fully expect to be hard at work with planning for hours afterward.

Though I will take a break between then and tomorrow night's raid. Mitch and I have a dinner date at home. We plan to cook together, and right now that seems like a very important thing to do. To spend a little time, just the two of us, before taking a leap into the unknown.

I need a touch of normalcy before everything goes sideways.

# 17

## Alexis

"Exactly how finely do you want these mushrooms chopped up?" Looking up from the cutting board, I wait for Mitch to turn away from where he's searing a beautiful hunk of beef tenderloin.

I know as soon as his nose wrinkles that I have work ahead of me. "Finer than that."

"Well, for heaven's sake. I should sear the meat so you can chop these mushrooms until they're practically a paste."

It doesn't matter how I protest. Mitch only laughs it off. "You want them as fine as possible, so when I put them in the pan, they cook into something close to a paste that goes all over the outside of the loin." And I was thinking cooking together would be relaxing.

Not that I would sincerely complain for anything in the world. It's fun, even when we bicker good naturedly like this. "So this is what your family used to eat every Christmas Eve?" I ask, returning to the mushrooms.

"Grandma made it every year," he replies while the meat sizzles in the cast-iron skillet. "It always seemed so special."

"I'm sure it did." If anything, I feel sort of guilty helping to prepare such an elaborate meal for just the two of us. Mitch's special mashed potatoes are next on the list, and we'll prepare those while the beef roasts.

Once he sets the meat aside to rest, I pretend to wipe sweat off my forehead. "I can't possibly get these mushrooms any smaller, boss."

"Nicely done." Then, while I watch, he chops up a shallot in a blur of the blade. My mouth falls open at how casually he manages to do it.

"Show off," I mutter, rolling my eyes while he laughs.

"Once I got to a certain age, I was in charge of prep work." While he cooks that down in the hot pan, I take a colander full of potatoes to the sink to rinse them off before peeling.

"Mom used to make these huge holiday feasts," I muse, smiling to myself at the memory. "Did I ever tell you about that?"

"Maybe, but I would like to hear it again." We exchange a smile, and he winks, and I am so grateful I was sent back here for work.

"She really went all Norman Rockwell," I remember. "The full feast. I remember a couple of years when both sets of grandparents came for dinner, but they moved down to Florida and didn't care for traveling during the holiday season. So before long, it was just the four of us. But Mom still made an insane amount of food."

"What are we talking about here? A turkey, a ham?"

"Try a large turkey, a small ham, and a baked ziti."

"Whoa. Pass the antacids," he groans.

"Then came the sides," I continue as I begin to peel. "Mashed potatoes, which is what made me think back of it in the first place. This was one of my first jobs, so the mashed potatoes weren't exactly perfect those first few years."

"I hope you've gotten better since then."

"You can peel them yourself, you know," I retort, making him snicker. "Anyway, there was also corn-bread stuffing, creamed spinach, roasted carrots. We would spend the next three or four days eating nothing but ham and eggs for breakfast and the other leftovers for lunch and dinner."

"That actually sounds pretty great. Something to hold onto, like a tradition."

As usual, he's found a way to deepen my under-standing and help me see things in a different light. "You're right. I never thought about it that way."

"It's not easy to hold onto those traditions when the generation gets, well, older," he muses while smearing Dijon, then the mushroom mixture on top of the beef. He sets it in the fridge to chill while he rolls out his homemade puff pastry, which is really the star of the show. He's been wanting to test new tech-niques for a while, since his homemade Danish is becoming a favorite at the café.

While he works on that, I take the peeled potatoes to the island so we can face each other. "Make sure you cut them uniformly," Mitch reminds me while sprinkling flour on the granite countertop.

"For real? Are you going to micromanage every aspect of this meal? I know how to dice potatoes for a mash."

"I'm just saying," he insists in a singsong voice. "Maybe you're a little rusty. You're out of practice."

"It's like riding a bike," I tell him, wearing a tight smile that makes him laugh before he dips his fingers into the flour canister and flings some across the island.

"You're going to get into a flour fight with a woman holding a knife?" I ask, narrowing my eyes. "That is a very bold move."

"Point taken," he concedes, laughing while he holds up his flour-dusted hands. "I know better than to fight with a lady holding a knife."

"Smart man." Though when he's not looking, I reach across the island and grab some flour to toss at him when he turns my way again. "There. Now we're even."

"You just get those potatoes right," he teases, pointing to the pot. "And let's be a little more efficient. Leave them out of water any longer, they'll start to turn black."

"Have I ever told you I love it when you get all commanding and what not?"

"Oh? Do you?" He lifts an eyebrow.

"Actually … yes, I do," I have to admit, giggling

harder than ever when he makes a move like he's going to chase me around the island. "I thought I had to get the potatoes on the stove before they change color!"

"Forget the potatoes," he growls, though he gives up the chase quickly.

"Wow." Clicking my tongue, I get back to work. "All talk, no action."

"I can't let you distract me," he chides, wagging a finger in my direction. "The pastry can't get too warm. Otherwise, you lose all the nice layers once it hits the oven."

"I would never want to get between you and your flaky layers."

I really wish I didn't have to leave tonight. It doesn't matter how much fun we're having or how many memories it stirs up, cooking together like this. Always, no matter what, there's a clock ticking. Counting down the seconds until I have to go on a very dangerous mission. I'm not looking forward to it —strangely enough, I am not at all eager to get out there and go in with guns blazing.

And I understand why in moments like this, doing something as mundane as putting a pot of potatoes to boil on the stove while Mitch wraps the beef in pastry before applying a pretty lattice on top. I have to applaud by the time he's finished painting egg wash over the whole thing. "I am impressed," I tell him. "Really. That's gorgeous."

"Don't worry. It'll be ready in plenty of time for you to go out later on." Clearly, I don't fix my face quickly enough, since he looks guilty when he catches sight of my expression. "Sorry. I didn't mean that the way it came out."

"No, it didn't come out any certain way at all. I understand." Though I do sort of wish he hadn't brought it up as I pierce a potato to test for doneness. But it's on his mind, and he doesn't have to pretend it's not. Not for my sake.

"How are you feeling about it?" His question is gentle, but I hear his curiosity. I understand it, too. He's not sure how far he can push or how much I want to talk about, and he doesn't want to take the wrong step.

"It's my job." I can only offer a shrug. "This is what I have to do. These are bad guys, and somebody has to stop them. I know," I add before he can, "I don't think all of it has to fall on me all the time. It just so happened I wound up in the middle of this."

"You end up in the middle of a lot of things," he points out while wiping down the counter.

"If it wasn't this case, it would be another." Stepping up behind him, I wrap my arms around his waist and give him a squeeze. "But I know what you mean."

I'm glad for the distraction of straining the potatoes and the chance to change the subject. Now it's time for him to begin the painstaking process of pressing the potatoes through a fine sieve. "Absolutely no lumps. That's my motto." He already has a small pot of cream, butter, and herbs keeping warm on the stove. It's fascinating, watching him lose himself in the preparation.

Finally, I have to ask, "Have you ever considered going to culinary school? Not just for baking, but for cooking in general?"

He chuckles before shaking his head. "You know what? I don't think I would like that."

"Why not?"

"Oh, you know." He lifts a shoulder, chuckling again. "I enjoy cooking. I like doing this to unwind. What a surefire way to lose interest in a hobby?"

"Make it your job?" I suggest, and we share a laugh.

"Exactly. This is fun, this is low stakes. I can be creative."

"So long as you keep it edible," I joke. "I'm an adventurous person, but there are limits."

"If there's one thing I aim for, it's making edible food."

The food is more than edible, as it turns out. By the time we sit down to the tender Beef Wellington, with its gorgeously brown, flaky crust, and potatoes so silky and rich I could cry, it seems pointless to ignore the elephant in the room. It's going on eight o'clock now, and we want to move in on the warehouse at midnight.

"It's not just me out there, either." I can't help but feel slightly jealous of the merlot Mitch enjoys with our meal. I could certainly use a little liquid courage a handful of hours before the raid, but it's the raid that's keeping me from drinking.

"You're thinking about the rest of your team?" he

asks, setting the wine aside, turning his full attention to me.

"Of course. The decisions I make affect them. They're all great, they all come with Agent Childs' full confidence. Still, what if?"

"What if what?"

"Just … what if?" I repeat with a helpless shrug. "Isn't that enough?"

He draws a deep breath which he then slowly releases. "I didn't know that was how you thought about the job. Don't get me wrong. I never assumed you romanticize it or anything like that. And I know you take it seriously when you have a team working with you. But I didn't know it weighs so heavily on you. I hate to see that."

"It's a necessary evil, I think. But that's all right. You know I can't imagine doing anything else."

"That much, I know." Still, he purses his lips thoughtfully before picking up his glass. "Though wouldn't it be nice to have a private therapy practice? Put that PhD to use elsewhere?"

"You know I would start itching for a little action the first day." All I can do is give him a shrug. "That's who I am."

"I wouldn't have you any other way," he assures me. Even so, his smile falters slightly. "Do me a favor and be careful. Can you do that for me? Promise me you'll be careful?"

"I will do my very best," I vow. And I will. I always do.

It's the bad guys I have to worry about.

# 18

## Alexis

The atmosphere is tense, the air practically crackling as I stand with Chief Perkins and Special Agent Childs a few dozen yards from where the rest of our combined teams perform last minute checks of their equipment, discussing entry plans. There are three potential entrances in total, including the loading dock. We'll have all three of them manned by officers waiting outside to snag any escapees while the Bureau team heads in with me and Agent Childs in the lead.

Who doesn't want their boss breathing over their shoulder at a time like this?

I can still almost taste the succulent meal I shared with Mitch earlier. It would've been so nice to clean up together, cuddle up in front of a movie, then go to bed. The way normal couples do, connecting after a long day at work. The best I can hope for is to find him in bed by the time I get home, although there's no telling how long it will take to process everyone and everything we discover inside that cinderblock building.

I can only hope for the next best thing, then. To go home to him safe and sound, like he needs me to be. It's the least I can do.

"We've counted seven vehicles parked around the building," I confirm, raising my voice to be heard. "There's a good reason to believe the suspect known as Viper is inside. He is our number one target, so keep an eye out for anyone resembling the images we've circulated among you."

Breath forms a fog around my head. I have to make a conscious effort to slow it down, to regulate my nervous system. I never used to get this way before a raid or any other similarly tense situation. What's changed?

That's a dumb question, one that almost makes me laugh. Before now, I didn't have Mitch. I didn't have something real, something with a future. I've also reconnected with Mom and Dad after years of estrangement. What happens to them if something happens to me now? They've both come so far, healing a little at a time now that they're back together. I don't want to destroy that.

"How are you holding up?" Special Agent Childs wears a probing expression, his eyes moving over my face in these final minutes before we split up in our vehicles and position ourselves around the building.

"Just fine. Can't wait to get in there," I tell him. Was I surprised that he decided to come out and join us? Not really. Disappointed, but not surprised. I wouldn't be able to sit back and wait for reports if I were in his position.

"How about you tell me the truth?" His voice is low enough that I know he can't be heard by anyone else, but that doesn't make it any easier to be questioned this way. I want to ask if he's posed the same question to any of the other agents, but I already know the answer. As it is, he has already warned me to take a step back whenever possible, to take care of myself after a harrowing stretch of weeks spent tracking down my sister's killer.

I can't have him thinking I've lost my nerve. Like I can't handle the job anymore.

Leveling a steady gaze, I repeat myself. "I can't wait to get in there."

His lips twitch, but that's as close as he comes to a grin. "Fair enough."

It's time. I give the signal for us to move out, gratified when the teams fall in line. What's even more gratifying is getting behind the wheel and approaching the warehouse after spending days observing from a distance. The ultimate goal is getting my hands on Viper, of course, but there's bound to be a treasure trove in there regardless of whether he's around tonight.

There's also bound to be countless weapons and a bunch of men ready to use them if it means saving their necks. The idea taps like Morse Code at the back of my mind as I park the car, then rush out to meet the others.

At a moment like this, the entire world drills down to a single point of focus. Yes, there are still night sounds all around me, the rustling of breeze through overgrown weeds, soft footsteps as we approach our destination. Without the benefit of many lights around, it's easy to see the stars.

All of that is a blur, background noise when compared to what's in front of me. A shadowy figure emerges from the south entrance and is immediately taken down by a bullet to the kneecap. By the time he draws breath to scream in pain, two of the local officers are on top of him, covering his mouth to keep him quiet while we continue inside.

The element of surprise doesn't last long. All it takes is a few cries of outrage from the men we find inside to raise attention. That's quickly followed by gunfire as one of their crew breaks out of his shock and raises his rifle.

It's better not to think. To rely on training, muscle memory. All of this has been drilled into my head for years, over and over, until it's second nature. I have to rely on that now as we move deeper into the warehouse, where crates and pallets are still arranged in clusters from one end of the building to the other, giving the enemy plenty of places to take cover.

The same is true for us. "Cover me!" I bark at Childs before darting ahead, staying close to the wooden crates, with my attention focused solely on a tall, dark figure running straight for a stairwell in the far corner.

"Viper!" I bellow over the cacophony of gunfire

and shouting around us. Hearing his name stops him for a second, makes his steps falter, but he throws himself through a door and disappears. I duck behind a crate when the whine of a bullet comes too close for comfort, then continue on, running at a crouch until I reach the door Viper disappeared through.

A pair of officers lie on the ground, both bleeding from wounds he must have inflicted. I sweep the area, watching for him, scanning the darkness as I approach the closer of the two. "Where did he go?" I ask, looking in all directions.

"Ran. Just ran. Don't … know … " The man at my feet groans and I glance down long enough to take in the red patch spreading across his stomach.

"Go on." The second officer drags herself over to him. "Just got me in the calf. No big deal. I'll take care of him."

"I'll send out more people to help you," I promise, looking around one more time before going in. One of our agents was wounded, sitting against the wall and drenched in sweat, but he shakes his head when I ask if he needs help. "Flesh wound," he manages through gritted teeth. "I know … we want them alive … but I aimed a little high when I returned fire."

"You just take it easy and don't worry about that." I have to move on, pushing my way back through the warehouse. Now, gunfire is nothing more than an occasional *tap, tap, tap*. Already, there's a handful of men in zip ties, some of them bleeding, all of them cursing us.

But not Viper. He got away again. Bile rises in my throat but I swallow it back, reminding myself there's more at stake than one individual. One of the rooms lining the warehouse's exterior walls catches my eye, its door open, the lights on inside. I duck in if only to catch my breath for a second or two, but all of that flies out the window once I understand what I'm looking at.

"We've got computers here!" Plenty of them, along with at least a dozen cell phones. Touching a hand to one of the chairs scattered around the room, I find it warm. Like whoever was managing the devices was working right up to the point where we came in. Communicating with suppliers? Arranging pickups and deliveries? The possibilities are endless, and from the looks of it, business has been booming.

"I need them carefully removed from the site," I bark at the closest agent once I step out of the room again. "Take every precaution. We can't afford to lose any of this to some chain of custody hang-up." My hands are twitching with the need to dig in and see what treasures the devices hold, but it's going to have to wait. This is only one room of many.

Once Childs finds me, we exchange a brief look that speaks volumes. He blows out a sigh. "Let's not lose hope. There is no way we don't track him down after finding all of this."

He's absolutely right, and I know it. No doubt we'll be able to unravel a lot of this enterprise once we access the machines I found. On top of that, I'm going home to Mitch later. Safe, in one piece, just as I promised.

I'll have to live with the gut-twisting resentment of knowing that maniac is still out there, running free.

*Not for long.*

# 19

## Alexis

"How are you feeling? Did you manage to get any sleep?" Chief Perkins rubs his bloodshot eyes before gulping down more of the coffee sitting on his desk.

"A little bit." Hardly any, really, but we don't need to get into specifics. I'm not going to describe how grateful I was to make it home and find Mitch asleep on the couch, waiting for me. He would have been getting up for work if I had been much later. We managed to have a few minutes together before he suggested we get a shower, then parted ways once he was dressed for the store and I was in a pair of pajamas I only pulled off and tossed aside just a few hours later. Part of me wonders if it wouldn't have been easier not to sleep at all, but I had barely been able to keep my eyes open by the time I arrived at the house.

Now, after stopping at the cafe for a very strong latte before my drive, I stood in the chief's office while a symphony of ringing phones and questions and conversation turned the station into something more like an overturned beehive. So much frenetic activity thanks to the presence of a dozen visitors down in the holding cells.

"We figured we'd let them cool off a little down-stairs before talking to them," the chief explains before gulping more of his fragrant brew. He smacks his lips before closing his eyes briefly. "I swear, there is not enough caffeine in existence. Now that the raid is over …"

"And the adrenaline has worn off," I conclude with a knowing chuckle. "I know. You felt like you could run through a wall last night, and now you want to curl up in a ball at the base of the wall and take a nap."

"Nap? I could use about twelve to fourteen hours of shuteye." His rueful laughter cuts off and is quickly replaced by a frown. "Of course, we still have two missing people out there."

Yes, we can't afford to celebrate our win when this is only part of the bigger picture. "I'm ready to start talking to these guys." Holding up what's left of my drink, I add, "Thanks in part to the fourth shot of espresso in my morning latte."

"I don't recognize the name on the cup. Is that a new place?"

"It's my boyfriend's cafe in Broken Hill." Pride surges in my chest. "He made me promise not to gulp all of it down on the way here. Too much caffeine to consume all at once."

"He sounds like my wife." He glances down at the

band on his ring finger. "I know she'll be glad once we find Ryan and Isabel and we can go back to our normal routine. This is actually a pretty quiet place otherwise."

Yes, but there's a beast lurking beneath that quiet surface. Now we know it, and there's no way to forget it. He will not be able to look away any more than I can. Finding Ryan and Isabel is now only part of the problem. This entire system needs to be dismantled one brick at a time.

Which means I need to get started with interviews. The chief instructs one of his deputies to bring the first man we booked up to an interrogation room. They'll all be tired after hours spent in the cells under glaring lights, unable to rest on the concrete benches lining the walls. I'm hoping that will soften the inevitable resentment and bitterness the men will be harboring after their arrests. Hours spent thinking over their actions and the consequences looming in front of them should—I hope—make them more willing to talk.

My hopes are dashed when the first, then second man demands a lawyer before he'll say another word. That's fine, of course. They have a right to do that, but it means more waiting. By the time I enter the room which holds the third detainee, I'm ready to walk right back out. Obviously, these guys are savvy enough to know what to say. The hours they'd spent cooling their heels may have meant them coordinating among themselves, forming a united front. My hopes are in the gutter by the time I take a seat across the table from the twenty-year-old kid who looks like he might have just started shaving yesterday and would easily fit in on a college campus with his baby face and wide eyes.

His knee bounces rhythmically, his heel tapping the floor like the ticking of a clock, only faster. "I don't know anything," he tells me right away, before I've had the chance to say a word or even confirm who I'm speaking with.

"George Bates?" I ask, confirming what I found in the folder hanging from a basket fixed to the interrogation room door. "Is that correct?"

He nods, gulps, and stares at me with bulging blue eyes. "Yeah, that's me. I'm telling you. I didn't even pull a gun last night. I'm not trying to get shot and killed. I've got a kid and my girlfriend, and I've been giving my mom money to cover her medications. That's all. I just needed to make quick money."

Bingo. I think I found a weak link. All I need is to apply the right amount of pressure, which means softening my gaze and clicking my tongue. "Listen, times are tough. People are doing things they never thought they'd have to do just to get by. I understand that."

"What do you want to know?" With a shaking hand, he brushes black hair away from his forehead. "Like I said, I don't know things. Nobody tells me much. But I do know names, if that helps. I can't let my kid grow up without a dad." It's the way his voice cracks that leaves my heart going out to him a little. According to the file, this is his first arrest.

"They don't have to, George," I murmur. "You've

never been in trouble before, and your cooperation will go a long way. You said you know names."

"Yeah, I do." There's hope in his voice now.

"How about Viper?"

A shudder runs through him and his knee bounces faster, hitting the underside of the table in a frantic rhythm. "Yeah. I know that name. We all do."

"He got away last night," I confirm, watching his expression turn to one of dismay and what might be pain, too. "Can you confirm his position in this organization? Where does he fall in the hierarchy?"

He holds a hand up above his head, palm facing the table. "Top of the pyramid," he replies. "I mean, that's how it seems. Everybody's always saying stuff like Viper said this or Viper wants to do that."

"Do you know his real name?"

"Nah. Maybe he doesn't have one." When I arch an eyebrow, he lifts a shoulder. He's sort of a scrawny kid, lanky, dressed in a faded T-shirt that looks like it's about three sizes too big. "I mean, I wasn't going to ask a question like that."

"Understood. How long have you been affiliated with this group?"

"I don't know. A few months, maybe? Since before Christmas. That's when Mom got diagnosed with diabetes. Her meds are insane."

I murmur my sympathy before asking, "Do you know of any other locations or safe houses used by Viper and the other higher ranking members?"

"I don't know. Really." He rubs his face with both hands before raking his fingers through hair long enough to brush his shirt collar. "My mom is going to be so upset when she finds out about this. I've never been in any trouble. Like I said, I just needed the money."

His choice of words inspires me to take another approach. "You know, we're looking into the disappearance of somebody we found out is affiliated with you guys. It could be he was in it for the money, too. I'm sure that's how everybody gets roped in. I wonder if you've ever met him."

"I don't know. There's a lot of people coming and going. I can't make any promises."

"This guy is in his 30s, professional type. An architect. I first got involved with the case surrounding the disappearance of him and his baby girl, which is what led me to you."

Light flickers behind his eyes. "What's his name?"

"Ryan McAlister."

His eyes widen a fraction. "Yeah, I know him." Out of nowhere, his demeanor changes. As annoying as it was, listening to his knee tap the desk, it's more unnerving when he goes still.

*Careful. Take it easy.* With my nails digging into my palms, I ask, "When was the last time you saw him?"

"Oh, I don't know. Maybe a couple weeks ago? I figured … " He lowers his gaze to the table, his jaw twitching but nothing coming from his lips.

"What did you figure?" I prompt. It takes all I have not to jump across the table, take him by his collar, and demand he tell me everything.

"Listen. I'm not saying I know any specifics. But

... I figured somebody found out what he was doing and, you know. Shut him up."

The words are barely out of his mouth before his head snaps up, his eyes darting over my face while the color drains from his. "I don't know anything. I'm gonna tell you that right here and now. I guess I assumed. But I don't know anything about where he went or what happened."

"What was he doing?" I can hardly breathe. The rapid drum of my heart is almost enough to deafen me.

"Listen. I don't know anything for sure, okay? But if I tell you this, will it help me? Like I said, I've got a kid," he murmurs. "I just wanna be there for him."

It isn't easy to keep from shaking visibly as I reply, "I will do everything I can to help you. You have my word, but I need to know everything you know."

"He handled a lot of stuff. When I first met the guys on this crew and started taking shifts at the warehouse, I used to see him sometimes. Product would come through, hidden in stuff he was ordering for his business. Like, supplies and stuff. That was how they hid everything in case there were any surprise searches or whatever. I don't know all the details," he adds with a wave of his hand.

It makes sense that they would use someone on the outside to legitimize their operation. So far, I find him plausible.

"But then ... " He takes a deep breath. "One day, I was gonna go home after an overnight shift watching the warehouse. It was early in the morning. This Ryan guy, he came in to talk to Viper about something. We were leaving at the same time, and ... I don't know. He was acting weird. Looking over his shoulder and stuff, typing on his phone on his way to the car. I was curious. I followed him to town—I still don't know why I did it. I should've gone straight home. He stopped and parked and went to this café, and I figured I would pick up breakfast and take it with me for my girl to have before she went to work at the store. And he was in there, Ryan, with somebody else. Sitting at a table."

"Who was this other person? Did you recognize them?"

He shakes his head. "They were writing something down, and Ryan was leaning in like he didn't want anybody to hear what he was saying. And he held out his phone—I don't know, maybe he didn't notice, maybe he never paid attention to me when we saw each other before. He didn't notice me walking past the table. But I saw what he was showing that guy, pictures he took in the warehouse. He was talking about a shipment and where it was going."

"What are you saying?" Thinking back on what he originally said about Ryan getting in trouble for who he was talking to, I ask, "You think he was feeding information to the authorities?"

"I don't know if it was the authorities or a rival or what. I just know he was giving information to somebody I never saw before. And then, he turns up missing. I saw it on the news."

"How long ago did you see the two of them talking?"

"A few weeks. I don't remember exactly when, but it wasn't all that long ago."

"Can you describe the person he was speaking to?"

He shrugs. "I don't know. Middle-aged. He was wearing a nice coat and a ball cap. Like, I don't know, maybe he didn't want to be recognized. But I didn't want to stare and have him recognize me."

"Sure. But what did your gut tell you?"

Immediately, he replies, "Reporter. He didn't look like a cop, and he didn't look like one of the guys I'm working with, you know what I mean? He was dressed nice and scribbling things down on a notepad."

The force of this revelation rocks me back in my seat. Ryan was speaking to somebody. Giving them information. Did it start out that way? Was he always intending to uncover this group's secrets? Or did someone get their hands on him once he was already in the belly of the beast?

No matter the reason why, I'm now looking at a man who may have faced the repercussions of his betrayal.

# 20

# Alexis

I wouldn't exactly say I'm dreading this. More like it's something I know I need to do but have been putting off for one reason or another. Too busy, mostly— though even when I have the time, I don't generally have the mental bandwidth to navigate a visit with my parents.

It was one thing to visit Mom or Dad on their own, when they were no longer living together. Sure, having them under the same roof is the same as killing two birds with one stone, metaphorically speaking. But it's twice the well-meaning but intrusive questions, two. And I know before I finish climbing the stairs up to the porch of the rambling old Victorian what the primary topic of conversation will be.

"You didn't bring Mitch with you?" Mom goes so far as to look over my shoulder, like she expects to find him ready to surprise her.

"I'm starting to think you like him more than you like me." I kiss her cheek before removing my jacket and hanging it next to the front door. "Or is it his pastries you love?"

Her wrinkled nose tells me I went too far. "You must have a very low opinion of me if you think that's what I care about."

"Sorry, sorry." Holding up my hands in front of me, I shrug. "We all know you really care about having grandchildren."

Her mouth opens. Her mouth closes. She pulls her handknit cardigan tighter around her thin frame. "Well, I won't pretend that hasn't come up in my thoughts from time to time."

"He had to stick around for a big delivery," I explain, letting her lead the way to the kitchen. "You know. Flour, sugar, coffee beans. There was a mix-up and they were supposed to deliver earlier this morning. It was either wait around tonight or have them come in tomorrow, but Mitch wants to set dough out to proof overnight." And I have officially offered too much information. I want to be sure she knows he wanted to be here, and that I wanted him here. I'm not trying to hide anything.

"He sure is devoted to his work." Mom lets out a sigh once we reach the kitchen, which smells of roast chicken, rosemary, lemon. "Something the two of you have in common."

"One of many things." I poke my head back out into the hallway before asking, "Where's Dad?"

"Oh, I have him going through some things in the basement. There were a bunch of unfinished projects down there from back when we were first working to renovate this place. He's sizing things up, seeing if there's anything worth finishing. It's incredible, really, how frozen in time I was for so long."

Amazing how she can deliver such a profound statement so easily, like she's not even thinking about it. She was frozen in time. So was Dad. So was I in a lot of ways.

And in some ways, I've started to thaw out. I'm even looking forward to the future. There was a long stretch of time when I didn't see a future in front of me at all—not that I didn't expect to live. I simply couldn't visualize beyond the dark, thick fog wrapped around me.

"There she is." The sound of Dad's chipper greeting squeezes my chest until it's hard to breathe. I could be ten years old again, doing my homework here while Mom cooks dinner and Maddie coaches me through math, which was never my strong subject. Incredible the way the past can come roaring back all at once, when a person least expects it.

"I'm a little tired," I explain when Dad looks at me with obvious concern on pulling back from our hug. "In the middle of a case. You know how it is."

"Then we are extra fortunate to have you with us for dinner tonight." He pats my cheek before offering a tiny smile. "Guess what I found in the basement? One of the old photo albums. I left it on the coffee table."

"So? How does it look down there?" Mom asks him as she checks the temperature of the chicken.

"Another twenty minutes or so," she decides before closing the oven door.

He makes an indecisive sound while washing his hands. "It's a mix. Some things aren't worth working on anymore, but there are a few standouts. I forgot all about that cabinet I was refinishing. I would like to haul that up to my workshop ... "

I love seeing them like this. Sure, it's still a little awkward at times. There's been a lot of water under the bridge, and I had gotten used to the idea of them never being together again. Not after all they had been through, both together and separately; Dad going to prison, Mom with her failed second marriage to a monster I can't bring myself to think about. That man drove a wedge between us and stole even more time we could have spent together.

When I think about him, the sight of her looking so happy and healthy with Dad is even more gratifying. I worried a little at first, once I got over the shock of finding out they would be living together again. Would they wind up hurting the other's sobriety? If anything, they both look and seem healthier than they were while apart.

But it would be a mistake to overlook the time that's passed. They're older now. The dreams they shared and worked on together have been put aside long enough that some of them just aren't worth taking out and dusting off at this point. What might have been? There never be an answer to that question.

"I'm going to go wash up," I announce, hopping

down from my stool and making a beeline for the powder room down the hall. It's tough to breathe all of a sudden. *I'll be okay. Everything is okay.* Tyler Mahoney is behind bars. I'm waiting to see what I can do to help Russell Duffy get out of prison.

It's only after I splash my face at the sink and take a few minutes to breathe that it hits me. How glad I've been ever since I got that call about a missing person's case outside Bangor. How convenient it is to be so absorbed in trying to find Ryan and Isabel, which of course led me to this drug ring.

If I'm absorbed in my work, there's no way for my unresolved issues to announce themselves.

An old coping mechanism, one I've genuinely tried to overcome. Using my job to block out reality is not a sustainable practice. I need to work through it, whenever the pain and regret bubbles up. Like right now, when I can't help but wonder if my inability to imagine a future had anything to do with guilt over being the one still alive. As if I couldn't imagine enjoying my life when Maddie couldn't enjoy hers.

I'm surprised Mom hasn't knocked on the door and asked if I'm doing all right, considering how long I've been in here. When I ease the door open, I hear the two of them bickering good naturedly in the kitchen over plans to continue renovating the house into a bed and breakfast. Maybe this time, they'll finally achieve their goal.

Rather than join them in the kitchen, curiosity leads me to the living room, where a thick photo album sits on the coffee table as Dad described. That was one of Mom's pet projects for a while, documenting the family.

It has been years since I've looked through this or, in fact, any of the albums she put together back in the day. Yet opening the cover to a photo of the four of us smiling from ear to ear in front of our Christmas tree brings back enough memories to almost choke me. It's like all of this has been waiting here for me to rediscover, frozen in time the way Mom described. I can smell the pine needles, can feel the popcorn between my fingers after spending hours stringing it on fishing line to make a garland that we draped over the branches. I learned very quickly how important it is to use a thimble. Nobody wants bloodstained garland on the tree.

But Maddie never pricked her fingers, just like Maddie was so effortlessly good at math and found it so easy to make friends and to fit in wherever she was. The way nothing ever seemed to get to her, a quality I had worshiped. She was my hero. Everything I wanted to be.

And we'll never know what she could have been. What right did he have to take her from us? From the world? A world that will only ever know her as a victim.

Photo after photo, memory after memory. My ninth birthday party. Maddie's fourteenth. Halloween —she stopped trick-or-treating when she turned twelve, but walked me through town for the next couple of years. She was always such a good sister. She didn't complain, didn't make me feel bad for taking her away from her friends for a few hours. When was the last time I thought about that?

Am I starting to forget her? Am I no better than the rest of the world, remembering her more as a victim than anything else?

It's not until a tear drips onto my chest that I realize I started crying. I close the album before I can ruin anything, holding it to my chest and sobbing silently, desperate not to let Mom and Dad know while they continue bickering and laughing together down the hall.

# 21

# Alexis

"You're heading in this early?" Mitch makes a big deal of checking his watch, frowning. "What's the big hurry? I know you didn't sleep well last night."

Exactly what I was hoping not to hear. "I kept you up, didn't I?"

He pulls on a long-sleeved tee before layering a polo with the shop's logo embroidered on the upper left. "It's not like I didn't go right back to sleep. Don't worry about it."

"You could take your own advice." Reaching up, I press a finger to the space between his eyebrows, where worry lines are etched deep. "Don't worry so much."

"Sure. It's that easy." He runs his hand over the back of my head before pulling me in for a hug which gives me the chance to inhale his soap and cologne. What I wouldn't give to be able to melt into him right now, to forget everything in favor of closing my eyes and being here, right here in this moment, where there's nothing but the two of us.

That's just not possible. My eyes open and I release a sigh that feels like it comes all the way up from my toes. "I guess dinner last night unlocked a lot of things. I didn't expect that photo album to make an appearance. It's like navigating a minefield sometimes. Just when you think the area around you is safe and free of danger … "

"Something blows up out of nowhere." He tightens his grip on me for a beat, touching his lips to the top of my head before letting me go with a sigh of his own. "I'm sorry. I wish I had been there."

"You can't shadow me wherever I go just in case something awkward happens." Though I do love him for caring as much as he does.

"At least come by the store for coffee and breakfast to take along with you."

Now, I can smile and mean it. "Who said that wasn't what I was already planning on doing?"

"I'm starting to think you're only with me because you like my muffins."

Standing on tiptoe, I brush my lips against his. "Now, that is just not true. I also love your lattes."

It's nice to leave for the day on a positive note, with Mitch's goodbye kiss lingering on my lips along with the taste of a blueberry muffin which I scarfed down before ducking out of the cafe. This is hardly my first early morning on the job, but there's a lightness in my heart that didn't exist before, back in the old days.

Amazing how I've come to think of that time as the old days when really, it's been six months since I moved back home. Six of the most eventful months of my life, granted, but only half a year. This time last year I was in Boston, a beautiful city, but nothing compared to what I see now as I drive out of Broken Hill to the field office in Portland.

First on my agenda this morning, checking in on our data analysts, gathering the information they've uncovered so far. I'm hungry for it, barely able to stay within the speed limit. It's especially challenging since traffic is so light at this time of the morning, when the sun hasn't yet breached the horizon. I want to fly down the road and dive headfirst into work, because work is safe. Even on days when the best I can do is spin my wheels and feel like I'm getting nowhere, at least I'm trying. At least there's a chance of finding the missing piece of a larger puzzle and clicking it into place.

Especially on a day like today, when our analysts have been working around the clock to uncover and decrypt files retrieved from the computers and phones found at the warehouse. I forwarded to Chief Perkins the message I received overnight, telling me some data has been retrieved and is ready for me to review. No doubt he'll be waiting with bated breath, which is exactly the way I feel right now as I count down the miles to go until I reach the office.

From the looks of it once I pull into the parking garage, I even managed to beat Agent Childs this morning. A handful of agents and technicians are heading out after their overnight shift, a couple of them lifting a hand in greeting as they pass me and my Corolla. I can't pretend not to prefer working out of this office, even if it's a little further from home. There's a different energy, a different mindset. Not that I hold anything against the local police department, but they simply can't touch what the highly trained and heavily funded analysts around here can accomplish.

And the evidence of that is plain to see once I take the elevator down to the lab. A trio of men around my age are hard at work at a series of long tables arranged in an H formation. Across the tables are set up the devices we recovered during the raid. Though I don't understand the lines of code flashing across the screens, I understand enough to know programs are being run on them.

A curly haired analyst wearing a pair of big headphones types rapidly enough on a keyboard that his fingers blur. Since he's the closest one to where I entered, I position myself nearby and wave a hand to grab his attention. "Oh, sorry." He slides the headphones away from his ears, letting them hang around his neck. "I was sort of in the zone. Agent Forrest, right?"

"Alexis, please. I couldn't stand to wait another minute to see what you dug up," I confess.

He nods toward an open box of donuts, four of which are left inside. "Want some breakfast? Help yourself."

"No, thanks." Though I do appreciate his generosity, this isn't a social call. "I got that taken care of before I left."

"Good enough." He shoves himself away from his desk, his wheelchair carrying him down the length of the table before he comes to a stop at the only laptop whose screen isn't covered in code. "Any clean files we manage to pull are being loaded onto this hard drive. If there's anything you want to look at, we only ask that you do it here rather than loading the files on a thumb drive or anything like that. There are still a lot of moving parts at work here and we want to keep a clean record of what we've extracted."

"Understood." I'm already reaching into my bag, retrieving my machine. I plan to keep notes on it, creating my own list of any names and locations I'm able to dig up. There must be a way to track Viper down now that we've chased him out of his hiding spot. There have to be others, so many others. Safe houses and hideouts, places for these criminals to get together and do their business. An operation of this size has to have them.

The analysts have been kind enough to sort the decrypted files into categories and place them in folders. *Bills of lading. Fuel and mileage. Shipping routes and schedules.* I have to admit, this is more organized than I expected for a common drug ring. They have fine-tuned their operation over time, that much is clear.

There's something else that catches my eye and makes my heart skip a beat before I open the folder. "Text threads," I whisper, trembling.

"Oh, yeah, the phones were a lot easier to get

into." The technician chuckles, gesturing toward my screen with the doughnut he just snagged from the box. "Sometimes, they try to delete the messages, like we can't just go in and retrieve them."

The hair on the back of my neck lifts as I start scrolling through the pages of messages, some of the threads going back six months, eight months, almost a year. A lot of it is what I would expect—plenty of check-ins, confirming arrival at a location, that sort of thing. These guys aren't exactly big conversationalists.

Scanning the lines of text, I search for addresses. Names. Phone numbers. Every time something inter-esting pops up I make a note of it on my laptop. V is mentioned more than once—no need to wonder who that is. They never type his full name. *V is mad. V says don't be late this time.*

GL. That's another pair of letters I see once, twice, half a dozen times as I continue skimming through the texts. *Stopped at GL. Dropped at GL.*

What is GL? I squeeze my eyes shut, going back through my memories of the ledger, the appointment book. Were those initials ever used?

Finally, I find it in a later text. Somebody used the full name, thank heavens. Golden Luck. When I plug the name into Google and add an area code, a listing for a Golden Luck Motel appears. Its low rating and rather dingy looking photos tell me this is probably the place I'm looking for. A rundown motel, somewhere I could have driven by half a dozen times and never noticed. It blends into the background, which I guess is what it's supposed to do. I doubt anybody stays there because their life is on an upswing.

Is this a safe house? Or is it simply a location where Viper knows there will always be customers eager to part with their money?

I guess there's only one way to find out.

# 22

# Alexis

"I would like to arrange surveillance on the motel." Standing in front of Agent Childs' desk, I clasp my hands behind my back. "Today."

"I see. We can arrange for that." I hear the reticence of his voice. His speech is slow, too, like he's working hard to make sure he doesn't say the wrong thing. I don't like the sound of it.

"But?"

A brief, pained smile touches the corners of his mouth. "But, we are barely a third of the way through the files on those computers. It's only a matter of time before anything that's worth recovering will be recovered. I cannot afford, literally or figuratively, to go off half-cocked and assign a surveillance team to this property when there could be another three properties even more critical to the ring's operations."

When my head tips back so I can stare at the ceiling tiles, he continues, "There needs to be a sense of proportion to all of this. We could be talking about some No-Tell Motel, where these guys stick their girl-friends, or crash when they're trying to duck their landlord. There's nothing in any of these messages to indicate this location's importance in the grand scheme of things."

"So you're telling me I can't have a team watching the place in case it's important."

Heaving a sigh, he confirms, "That is the long and short of it, yes."

"Then I would like to go on my own."

His eyes slide shut, a muscle in his cheek twitching before he mutters, "How did I know you would say that?"

"I feel it in my gut. This place is important. I can't explain why, but that's the purpose of surveillance, right?"

I hold his gaze for the time it takes my heart to beat once, twice, until he gestures toward one of the chairs beside me. "Have a seat."

"But—"

"Humor me." Clearly, he's not taking no for an answer. I'll do as he asks, though the clock ticking in the back of my head gets a little louder all the time.

There's nothing relaxing about settling into the leather club chair. I'm about three seconds away from jumping out of my skin, ready to race down the road and not stop until I end up at that motel. I need to know why it's important. Is Ryan there? Would someone there know where I can find him now?

"I understand we haven't worked together very long," he begins with a sigh, folding his hands on top of the desk.

The overhead fluorescent light makes his complexion look sallow, unhealthy. I shudder to think what it's doing to me, considering the bare minimum of sleep I've been surviving on this week. "And while the reports from your superiors in Boston were nothing but glowing, there is a common thread running through them. Something familiar, like the baseline of a song. And that baseline tells the story of someone with a penchant for obsessions."

"Obsession?" He doesn't react to my disbelieving laughter.

"The word itself may not have been used, but there are ways to get an idea across without spelling it plainly. Why do you think I encouraged you to take time to yourself after everything you went through in Martha's Vineyard and in North Carolina?"

Thinking back on the hike with Mitch, I argue, "I took a little time for myself."

"Agent Forrest, you took a day off. One day." He holds up a finger. "That is not what I had in mind, and I think you know it."

"In the middle of an investigation? Am I really being dressed down for dedicating as much of myself as I can?"

"That's just it." Now he looks sad, which somehow is worse than anything I've seen from him so far. "You are a dedicated agent. But burnout is real. Don't tell me somebody with your credentials doesn't know that."

My skin prickles uncomfortably, and the effect only worsens when he narrows his eyes and practically stares holes through me. "I would rather lose you for a week or two than see you take a six-month sabbatical that turns into a year. It happens. More than you know. I don't want to see you reach that point, and I know you don't, either."

Waving a hand, he indicates my appearance. "Respectfully, you look like death warmed over."

"Respectfully, of course," I murmur, making him snicker.

"I don't want to offend you. I want to get through to you," he insists. "It is critically important that we move fast, but I have to keep our resources in mind. And I have a boss, too," he reminds me with a roll of his eyes. "I can't justify assigning agents to a surveillance detail when there could be a much more pressing discovery around the corner. We need to gather all the information, then make a plan based on it."

The problem is, I know he's right. I don't even have to search very deep down inside myself to find the truth behind his words. There isn't a doubt in my mind he's already gotten more than an earful from his superiors about effective use of manpower, efficiency, all the other buzzwords so often used in our line of work. Men and women who have been sitting behind desks and in meetings for too long. Long enough that they forget how much of this job is instinctual, how much it involves working from a gut feeling. Exploring leads, meeting people, asking questions. Making decisions from higher up means missing the small details.

And it's those details which can make or break an entire case.

What do I want out of this? To get out of here and get eyes on that motel. Viper must have gone somewhere. Even if he's not there, I have a feeling there are others who might know him – or know how to find him.

If I'm going to get what I want, I need to play nice. It helps that I genuinely like and respect the man sitting in front of me. I feel for him, too, I do. It can't be easy, sitting on the fence between his agents and his bosses, trying to keep everybody happy while also being an effective agent.

"I will take a look at this place on my own," I offer. "Just me, by myself, casual surveillance. I only want to get a feel for the people there. Is this a safe house? Are they storing product there? Other substances like firearms, maybe? I want to get a sense of it. That's all."

His nostrils flare as he takes a deep breath. Did he think he was going to shut me down that easily? He's right. We haven't worked with each other for very long. "Have you forgotten where this case started? What do you think this is going to do to bring Ryan and Isabel home? That's an honest question," he adds when I groan softly.

The leather squeaks when I sit up, leaning in, tapping a finger against the desk. "This is the key. Ryan was working with these people. We have reason to believe he was also feeding information about the drug ring to a third party. Did Viper find out somehow? Did he have Ryan silenced? Is there someone even higher up in the organization we haven't yet learned about? Let's face it," I conclude. "This is the strongest connection we have to what became of this man. He would hardly be the first person who ever got caught up in something much bigger than they imagined. If I have to learn every single detail of this operation to track down the McAllisters, that's what I'm going to do."

My chest rises and falls rapidly by the time I'm finished. I didn't realize how worked up I was until now, when the sudden silence filling the room contrasts sharply with the flood of words that just poured out of my mouth. Did I say too much? Was I too passionate?

Maybe, but he doesn't seem to mind. "All right. You've made your case. But you will have to go alone."

"I understand." Frankly, this has to stay under the radar. After a raid like the one we conducted two nights ago, these people will be on edge. Looking over their shoulders.

"I expect regular reports," he adds when I stand.

"And you'll get them. Thank you." It's probably a good idea to get out of here before he changes his mind.

I spent hours down in the lab, painstakingly digging my way through countless messages. My eyes are glad for a break from scrolling through so much text. I still have plenty of hours of daylight ahead of me, though, and I set off feeling energized in a way that no amount of caffeine can touch.

I'm getting closer. I feel it. It's only a matter of time now.

Along the way, I call Mitch to let him know my plan. "I'll be perfectly safe," I conclude, hearing his soft sigh but pretending not to. "I'm only watching a motel. There are other businesses to either side, and a couple across the road. I can park in one of their lots and not be noticed."

"But you said it looks pretty sketchy from the photos you saw."

"It does," I admit. "But it's nothing I can't handle. And again, I'm not going to be parking in front of the front office and interrogating people as they come and go. I'm only watching."

"For what? That's what I don't understand." The murmur of voices in the background cuts off, telling me he ducked into the kitchen or his office. It's 12:30 now, meaning there are probably customers in for the lunch rush. I hate to take him away from them, but then I'm not the one starting an argument.

"For anything that looks out of the ordinary. This Viper guy. He could be there."

"Or he might not be. Then what?"

"Then something else. They could be storing product there—a couple of the messages I read said something about drop-offs and pick-ups. I could catch signs of merchandise coming in or going out. That would be all I'd need to get a warrant."

For a while, there's nothing but the sound of his breathing mixing with my own. "I just think you're getting too far away from the original point of all of this. Finding that baby and her father."

"I hear you." Because I do. And it isn't as if I haven't already asked myself similar questions, reminding myself where this started. Of the mother and son still waiting at home, losing a little more hope every day. Every time the phone rings and it isn't news of Ryan and Isabel. "They have to be the people behind it, whatever happened. I feel it in my bones, Mitch. Do you trust me?"

"Always," he responds without hesitating. "That's never the problem. It's everybody else I don't trust."

"Which is why I'm going to stay at a distance." And I will, since I have no desire to announce myself and blow the whole thing to pieces. It wouldn't do me much good if these people knew there was an agent watching from across the road. "I will be perfectly safe, and I'll keep you posted."

All he does is grunt in response. I guess that's going to have to be enough. I can't tell him how to feel – and there are much worse things in this world than having somebody who cares enough to worry.

# 23

# Alexis

I admit, I didn't know what to expect on my arrival at the location ten miles outside town, where a motel even more depressing than the photos currently posted online sits along the stretch of road that was once a major thoroughfare for truckers, but was bypassed by the interstate decades ago. I imagine the traffic was much heavier back in the day. There was more need for the motel across the road, the diner beside it which now sits abandoned, a gas station with Out of Order signs on two of the three pumps. In other words, the surroundings are rather bleak. Even so, I'm glad when night falls, concealing me in shadow while I sit in the parking lot of a convenience store.

The convenience store is … well, convenient. There's a restroom inside, which is not exactly sparkling clean, but not so dirty I wouldn't consider using it. Every snack food imaginable is at my finger-tips. I'll stay here another few hours before moving the car to the parking lot of an adult bookstore three doors down from the motel. I never did understand places like that, especially with the rise of the internet. Yet all throughout the afternoon and evening, cars have pulled in and out of the lot in front of that windowless building.

I came into this with a few expectations, which makes what I find after the first several hours of surveillance that much more surprising. It isn't a bunch of armed men I've witnessed moving between rooms, having conversations in front of half-open doors, getting in and out of cars.

It's young women. Young women who look like they might live at the motel—one of them steps out in a tank top and a pair of cut offs, walking barefoot across the concrete running in front of the rooms to fill an ice bucket at a machine at the far corner of the U-shaped structure. As she returns to her room, another young woman steps out from behind another door and lights a cigarette, leaning against the wall before exhaling a cloud of smoke. She looks tired, worn-out. Worried. Even from a distance, I recognize the strain on her face.

That isn't what makes my heart stutter when another one of the doors opens around seven o'clock. Night has fallen, and what little traffic there was has slowed down further. Sound carries better without cars passing on the road between where I sit, and where the young woman who got the ice earlier on now paces back and forth in front of a room, gently bouncing a crying baby.

All the air leaves my body in one breath. It's like a

punch to the stomach, finding a baby in the middle of all of this. It changes things. Is this the only baby in that motel? These other women, do they have children, too?

If I listen hard enough with the window cracked, I can hear the faint sounds of the baby crying. I don't have much personal experience with babies, but what I hear sounds normal. Not the kind of crying that signals illness or injury. The girl pats the baby's back, and soon the sound quiets before the baby rests her head on the girl's shoulder.

How old is she? An infant, by the looks of it. What are the chances …

No. I can't afford to craft wild theories with no facts to back them up. It's a coincidence, that's all, having a baby there who might be around the same age as Isabel. Right? Regardless, the idea of going in there with weapons drawn is off the table. Not unless I know for sure there are no kids inside those rooms.

As per our agreement, I give Special Agent Childs a quick call to catch him up. "I'm switching locations shortly," I conclude. "As of right now, I'm starting to wonder if the women here work within the ring."

"Trafficking?"

"Affirmative. I've seen a few men arrive, then leave roughly thirty minutes later. For the most part, though, I've only seen the women coming in and out. Chatting, going to the vending machine. Once or twice, I saw one of them cross the road to duck into the convenience store."

"Businesses like that are a refuge for people who

can't afford to do more than pay week by week," he muses. "People are down on their luck. A motel like the one you're describing is perfect—nobody asking questions, everybody generally minding their own business."

"Exactly. I haven't seen much movement from the front office," I add, staring in that direction. A neon sign flashes over the scarred door leading inside. *Vacancy*. The *No* is darkened. "I'm sure they don't mind looking the other way, either."

"Any sign of our guy?"

The question leaves a bitter taste in my mouth. "No. I've seen a handful of questionable looking men since I got here. But not him."

After promising to check back in another couple of hours, I end the call, then remove my ball cap and run my fingers through my hair. My body is stiff after sitting in the same position for hours, only taking short breaks to visit the store. This is not the most exciting work—more than once I have to fight off a yawn, struggling to avoid the boredom and fatigue threatening to overwhelm me. This was a better idea earlier in the day, when I felt fresher. I'm not giving up, but that doesn't mean it's easy to stay focused.

I need to. What happens if I miss something? More cars come and go at the motel now, so at least there's something to change up the routine of the last few hours.

The interactions I'm witnessing take on a different tone. There's more looking around after someone gets out of a car, for instance, and I notice more than one gun tucked into a waistband. One of the guys leaves a room carrying a backpack he did not enter with. Obviously, they're doing business out of this place. I make a note of it, then jot down what I can make out of the license plate.

It's a surprise to see Mitch's name on the caller ID when my phone rings, but when I notice it's now past ten o'clock, I understand why he's calling. And there I was, getting bored hours ago, afraid of drifting off to sleep. This uptick in movement across the road has me in its grips.

"Hey there," I murmur on answering through the car's Bluetooth. "How's it going? Packing it in for the night?"

"That's exactly what I was about to ask you," he replies in a voice heavy with concern. "Are you still out there?"

"Yes, and I meant to switch locations ages ago. I need to change things up before somebody notices me." As it is, there's a pair of men standing beside a gray truck now, smoking cigarettes, occasionally looking this way. Are they looking at me? How obvious would it appear if I moved right now?

"You could try coming home for the night, you realize. You left the house before dawn."

"I know I did." Yes, I think I've been spotted. "I'm sorry, and I'm more than ready for you to holler at me later, but right now I have to go."

"Alexis, would you listen to me for once? We're looking at a sixteen-hour workday here, and you have no intention of leaving anytime soon. This is unhealthy."

"Childs doesn't want to assign anyone else to this," I explain, gripped by indecision as I lower the brim of my cap, concealing most of my face. "Which means I am the only person able to do this now. The women at that motel, the men who keep coming and going. Something is happening here."

"Something you are not going to be able to stop on your own, Alexis. Whatever happened to remembering you are not the only agent in the entire FBI?"

"I'm sorry. I really am." Now one of the men moves away from the truck, walking to the curb and stepping off it. Heading my way. Do I stay? Do I pull away and risk being followed? For all I know, he could be crossing the road to pick up another pack of cigarettes.

Just to be on the safe side, I press my fingers to my temples before waving my hands wildly enough for him to see. "I can't come home right now," I tell Mitch, mouthing a few other words for the sake of the man drawing closer with every step. My windows are rolled up, and I can only hope the act comes across believably.

"There's a difference between can't and won't." He ends the call and I make a big deal of smacking my palm against the steering wheel before covering my face with my hands. *Let him buy it. Please, let him buy it.*

It's not another moment before there's a sharp rapping against my window. I jump, eyes wide, looking out to find a scrawny kid who reminds me of George Bates bent at the waist, peering in at me. Unlike baby faced George, this kid is hard. Sharp. "What are you doing out here? You a cop or something?"

I roll down the window a bit, shaking my head. "Listen, I came out here after I had a fight with my boyfriend, and I'm trying to cool off, okay? I just got off the phone with him. Can you not get on my case, too?"

He holds up his hands, snorting. "Okay, whatever. You look a little shady, is all. But you better leave anyway," he adds, looking toward the store. "They don't like people being out here for long. They might call the cops, have them come and tell you to go. We don't need any of that across the road, get what I mean?"

Oh, I get what he means. I'm tempted to arrest him and take him in for questioning, but that would only scare off everybody else currently at the motel. One step at a time. "Yeah, gotcha." A sigh of relief eases its way from between my pursed lips once he continues on into the store.

Mindful of his friend, I hang a left on exiting the lot and start down the road. With my attention on the rearview mirror, I drive at a steady pace, watching to make sure a certain truck doesn't swing out of the motel parking lot and follow me.

I'm a mile down the road before I can breathe easier, then another two miles further down before doubling back. Rather than approach the motel, I park behind the adult bookstore with the intention of continuing to the motel on foot. The businesses along this strip share one giant parking lot with nothing but a few concrete dividers to keep cars from cutting through its entire length. Not that anyone would need to do that when traffic along the road is so thin and sporadic.

Before getting out of the car, I wait to see if the gray truck leaves. Not ten minutes pass before it does, traveling past the bookstore and continuing on until the tail lights blink out into darkness. Now I remove my cap, taking off my jacket and grabbing a pair of sunglasses from the glove compartment. I don't think the kid who approached me at the convenience store would recognize me now, considering so much of my face would've been shaded by the brim of my cap.

That doesn't mean I'm not careful as I step out of the car and sling my purse over my shoulder. I have to get closer. I have to find out why those women are there and how they fit into all of this.

Even if it means getting way too close for comfort.

## 24

## Alexis

Stepping through the front door of the motel's office is like stepping back into a time before I was ever born. I have seen enough movies and TV to recognize the furnishings coming from somewhere in the late 80s, when mauve was a big color. The carpeting might have been a pretty shade at one time but has been worn down to the padding in some places and hopelessly stained everywhere else. The pervasive odor of greasy food permeates the air, and that blinking neon sign out front casts a reddish glow through dirty windows.

A large, broad-shouldered woman sits behind the counter, flanked by several bouquets of dusty silk flowers arranged in vases. "Can I help you?" she asks, looking me up and down and not bothering to hide it. She's what Mom would call a bruiser, somebody I would not want to tangle with.

"I hope so," I tell her with a shy smile as I approach. "I need a room for the night."

Again, she studies me, her deep set eyes narrowing to slits. "Who sent you over here?"

An interesting way to phrase the question. "Nobody? I just need a place to stay for the night and it says outside that you have vacancies."

"The sign's broke. That's why it blinks like it does. It should say No Vacancies." Staring at me, she adds, "Sorry about that. Good luck to you."

I have been officially dismissed. Well, it was sort of a longshot, anyway. "Oh. Okay, thanks anyway." The truth is, I don't mind leaving the office, and not because I can practically feel the odor in the air soaking into my clothes. I don't like the entire vibe this woman gives off. It wouldn't surprise me if there were a shotgun behind the desk. If this is the kind of business it appears to be from the outside – the sort of place where unsavory and even criminal activity takes place—she's going to be wary of random newcomers showing up out of nowhere.

And she's going to want to protect herself. I can't imagine any amount of money being worth that kind of constant apprehension, always being on the defensive, but then I guess people don't think about what's going to come up further down the road when somebody offers them a lifeline. They probably told her it would mean more business on a fairly dead stretch of road. She might have seen Viper and his crew as the answer to a prayer.

It's a cool night, and I shiver slightly in my long sleeved polo and jeans as I wander slowly from the office. Instead of heading out toward the road, though, I walk in the opposite direction, toward the corner where two sides of the U-shaped structure meet. The ice and vending machines sit in a little vestibule, beyond which is the back parking lot which is empty aside from broken glass and a few scattered trash bags.

Over the hum of the machines I hear a door open behind me. It's the girl I saw earlier, holding the baby. Her arms are empty now, but there are a few bills clutched in one hand.

"Hi," I offer as she approaches. She's on the younger side of the age range I had in mind, early twenties at most. Her long, reddish blonde hair looks darker now that it's wet, hanging loose around her shoulders. She's bare faced after her shower, which might be why she looks a little younger, too.

She barely glances my way, her lips hardly forming the suggestion of a friendly smile, now folding her arms in front of her stomach before coming to a stop in front of one of the vending machines.

"I was trying to get a room here," I murmur, drawing closer. "But the lady in the office said there weren't any rooms open. Do you think that's true? It seems pretty empty. I don't get it."

She lifts a shoulder beneath her oversized t-shirt. "I don't know," she mumbles before feeding the bills into the machine and punching two of the buttons.

Then she taps her fist against the glass. "Man! I hate it when it does this!"

"Did it get stuck in there?" This is my chance to form a connection. Sure enough, a bag of corn chips dangles from the end of the row. "I hate that. Here, I'll help you rock the machine a little."

"Pearl will be so mad," she whispers, looking over her shoulder toward the office. Pearl. Somehow, the name shouldn't fit, but it does.

"That's why we're only going to have to rock it one time," I whisper back. "And then, we can hide back here behind the building in case she comes out to see what the noise was." Though honestly, if half of what I've already imagined takes place around here, I would think she'd be used to ignoring sudden noises. The woman would never sit still otherwise.

We stand at opposite sides of the heavy machine. "I'll push first, then you push back," I whisper. "One, two, three."

Like magic, the corn chips drop into the slot. She is smart enough not to reach for them, even giggling as we duck around the corner, out of sight. We hardly made a sound and I doubt Pearl would've heard with eight rooms between her office and the vending machine, but who's to say?

After a few moments, I peek around the corner. "I don't think she heard," I announce.

The girl giggles again. "Thanks. I'm starved." She returns to the machine and reaches inside for the chips, while something about her choice of words brings up a question.

"Why not just go across the street? They have corn chips over there, I bet." I know they do, in fact. They're probably cheaper than the price on the machine.

"Oh. I can't right now." She starts inching backward, tucking her hair behind her ear, biting her lip. "I better get back to my room. Thanks for the help."

"Wait, please. I'm looking for someone," I whisper. "That's why I wanted to get a room here, because I was hoping he was here, too. Maybe you've seen him."

Her eyes widen in the dim light from the few overhead bulbs still working. "I have to——"

"It's all right," I insist, smiling, doing everything I can to be gentle and friendly. "I swear, I'm only here looking for this guy. Early thirties, good looking, dark hair. I think he was wearing a blue plaid coat or jacket," I add, remembering the fabric I found caught on his truck.

When she ducks her head, I add, "I was only wondering if you ever saw him here. Or if you know somebody who has."

She doesn't say a word, but she doesn't run, either. Eyeing the bag of chips, I decide to take another direction. "How about I buy you something else from the machine to go with the chips? You said you were starving. That's not enough. What about a drink to go with it, even?"

Is this an act of desperation? It could be but, also gets through to her, lifting her head until her wide, dark eyes meet mine. "Really?"

"Whatever you want. My name is Alexis," I add, holding out a hand. "What's yours?"

She hesitates a moment before giving me a handshake. "Keaton. I'm not in any trouble?"

"Not at all."

"Is he in trouble? The guy you're looking for?"

"It's what I'm afraid of," I admit with a sigh.

"I did see him around here." Her head bobs slightly. "I think his name was Ryan something."

Did I offer to buy her whatever she wants? I'll buy her everything those machines hold.

# 25

# Alexis

One thing is abundantly clear by the time Keaton pops open a small bag of pretzels to go with the chips she's already nearly finished—the girl wasn't kidding when she said she was hungry. Rather than take a few pretzels out by hand, she tips the bag into her open mouth and pours them inside.

I uncap a bottle of water and hand it to her, waiting for her to swallow, almost ready to jump off the curb we're seated on. I need her to come out with the full story, and there's not much time for her to do it. The last thing I need is to spook her, though, and scare her into silence. She needs a friend now. She's just a kid.

"Thank you for this," she mumbles, chewing. "I didn't remember until a little while ago that I forgot to eat today."

"Then I'm glad I was here. How come you didn't eat? Are you having trouble? Do you need help?" At the end of the day, this case goes way beyond Ryan and Isabel. There is an entire world of misery I've only begun digging into.

"No, I don't need help." Sure, that was very believable. She doesn't seem terrified at all.

"You said you saw Ryan around here?"

Her head bobs before she takes a swig of water. "Yeah, but it's been a little while. A week, maybe? The days all seem the same sometimes, you know?"

"Why was he here? Do you know?" She shakes her head with a shrug before opening a bag of cookies. "How many times did you see him? Can you remember?"

"A few times. He sort of, you know. Sticks out. Like some random, normal guy hanging around here." Snickering, she takes a few cookies from the bag and almost shoves them in her mouth. "We don't see a lot of those."

"So he's not the sort of person you normally run into at the motel."

"Uh, no." There's something deeply jaded in the way she snickers again. She's too young to be so jaded. "But like I said, it's been a while since he was around here."

She's hiding something, and she's not doing a very good job of it. Sometimes, a subject will spill their guts without much prompting, almost like they were only waiting for the opportunity and are glad to finally have it. People who can't stand the weight of the secret they're carrying, who can't help but set that burden down the second they see an opportunity.

Keaton is not one of those people. I doubt she's

doing it to be difficult, the way some people do. Those who take pleasure from jerking law enforcement around, making everybody dance to their tune. A way of feeling powerful after a life of feeling anything but.

No, this girl has a reason for clamming up. Her cheap, rubber flip-flop taps on the ground in an increasingly quick rhythm. Her gaze shifts back and forth until I'm compelled to look behind me, wondering if someone is watching. "Is everything okay? You seem very jumpy."

She sits up a little straighter, like a kid in school trying to prove to the teacher they're really paying attention. "No. I mean … you know."

"No, I don't. Explain it to me, please. Maybe I can help."

Another snicker, softer this time. Almost tinged with pity. "It's fine. I shouldn't even be talking to you, but you know that."

"So why are you?" I whisper, because I might as well take a chance.

She takes her time picking the last of the cookies out of the bag. "I don't know. Because of the baby, I guess."

My entire body is vibrating, my gaze focused solely on the girl in front of me. I'm so close, with answers just beyond my fingertips. If I try too hard, I could erase all the progress we've made. "There's a baby? Where? What do they have to do with it?"

"I don't really know. Somebody brought her here while I was asleep one day. I can't remember, but I guess it was sometime last week. She's cute. Really little."

"How little?"

"Well, it's not like she could tell me," she points out, a little sour. "Just really small. We've kind of been taking care of her. Working in shifts, you know? She's asleep right now."

"That's why you didn't want to go across the street to get food." I had a feeling, but now I know.

"Yeah. One of the other girls is with her now, too, but she's going to wonder what's taking me so long. I really better get back."

No, no, there's so much more I need to ask her. Now that she's eaten, though, I wonder how much more she'll tell me. She's nervous enough as it is, bouncing on the balls of her feet once she stands and wipes her hands on her shorts.

"Do me a favor." Looking around one more time, I hand her my card once I'm sure it's safe. "Call me if anything unusual happens."

"Unusual?" She arches an eyebrow but takes the card. Slowly, but she takes it.

"If it seems like something's happening, if there's a lot of excitement or tension or anything out of the ordinary. Please, call me."

"Sure." I don't know if she means it. I only know I have no choice but to let her go back to her room. I make a note of which one it is, watching until she closes the door.

Now that she's gone, the adrenaline that was holding me together begins to subside a little. It has to be Isabel in that room. What are the odds of another small baby being held here? A baby Keaton doesn't know.

Hers is the fifth room from where I'm standing. I walk around the outside of the structure counting what I assume are small bathroom windows. The fifth window sits partly open. There's a TV on inside the room, the volume low enough that I hear Keaton's flip-flops snapping with every step she takes. The bathroom light flips on and I hold my breath, standing very still. Soon, it's clear she's brushing her teeth, and a minute later the light turns off again.

When soft, high-pitched whimpering reaches my awareness, my heart seizes. Isabel. There is no way this is a coincidence. Why is she here? Where did Ryan go? Is he ever coming back, or has somebody made sure he won't?

"Quiet down," a woman groans. The other woman Keaton mentioned, though she never used a name. "I'm trying to sleep."

A moment later, the bathroom light flips on again, and the baby's whimpers get louder once Keaton brings her into the room and closes the door. "It's okay, baby. You're safe here." She makes soft shushing noises, giving me the sense that at least Isabel is being cared for—but she needs her mother. For one crazy second, I imagine asking Keaton to hand her over. Maybe I can get through to her, explain the situation.

No, it would be too risky. The girl is too jumpy, too worried about what will happen to her. I can only imagine what she has been through, how much she's sustained. What she has seen.

I know what I need to know. That knowledge gets me moving across the paved lot, back to where I left the car. Once inside, I can release the breath I was holding, letting my head fall back against the seat while I review what I know so far. Whatever's going on in there, I'm going to need backup to uncover it. Not only for my sake, but for Isabel's. This is going to take caution at every step. That's why I call Chief Perkins.

"I have major updates for you." Quickly, I run down the details while he listens in silence. "What's your relationship like with a local PD around here?" Because according to maps, this is just beyond his jurisdiction. I don't particularly feel like getting held up in a bunch of politics between one department and another, but I have to go by the book.

"Jim Sheridan's a good guy," he tells me. "I'll call over there, let them know. That motel has been a thorn in everybody's side for a long time. An open secret from what I understand. Never been able to clear it out for long before the same type of people come back."

"So long as management encourages it, or at least looks the other way, there's nothing to stop him."

"Well, that's going to change now. This could be what they need over there to make a difference. He'll be happy to join in with us."

"I'll keep surveillance," I decide, staring at the building through my windshield. "Make sure everyone involved remembers there is an infant involved in all of this. We will need a wide perimeter. No lights, no noise."

"With respect, Agent Forrest, we know what we're doing."

I can't afford to worry about his hurt feelings when I heard that baby in that room. I was only feet away from her, with a cinderblock wall between us. Her mother is waiting for her at home, desperate to have her baby back. I want so much to call her, to grant her a little bit of peace, but instead I sit and wait, knowing it won't take long for back up to arrive once Chief Perkins gets the ball rolling.

"It's all right, Isabel," I whisper, staring at the light glowing behind that tiny bathroom window. "It will all be over soon. I promise."

# 26

# Alexis

The bathroom light has been off for quite a while by the time the cars arrive, spread out across the length of the parking lots behind the row of businesses flanking the motel. There are a few parked outside the adult bookstore, out of sight of the motel, while others park behind the empty diner. Unmarked cars, all of them, arriving one and two at a time. My nerves are shredded by the time Chief Jim Sheridan confirms all units are in place.

Along with Chief Perkins, we stand beside my Corolla, going over the plan. "I'll go in first, in case Keaton answers the door. She trusts me," I explain. "She'll recognize my face. I might be able to coax her out with the baby before anyone else goes in."

"And if she doesn't answer?" Chief Sheridan asks, hands on his hips as he eyes the motel. He's a tall, wary, no nonsense sort of man. "What then?"

"I try to appeal to whoever does answer," I decide. "There's another woman. I might be able to get through to her, to convince her to give up the baby. I can give her my word you'll go gentler with her if she cooperates."

"Are you in the habit of making promises for others, Agent Forrest?" Chief Sheridan asks.

"I'm in the habit of saying whatever needs to be said if it means freeing an infant before she's caught in the crossfire." I hold his gaze for a few endless, uncomfortable beats before he looks away. "I know, it's not ideal. And I am not in the habit of making promises I can't keep," I add, lifting my chin. "But that baby is in there, and these people are going to be desperate. I need to get her out."

"We're talking about a baby less than a month old, Jim," Chief Perkins reminds him. "We can't waste the opportunity to get her out of there unharmed."

"From what I've seen, it looks as though everyone is in for the night," I continue. "There's minimal chance of other parties arriving—there haven't been any cars in or out in over an hour, closer to two," I inform them, checking my phone to confirm. "I've only seen people emerge from three of the rooms, including the one in question. The ones on either side, as well. Most of the other rooms are dark. I haven't been able to tell whether there's anyone inside but there are a handful of vehicles parked in front of the rooms. They could be sleeping off a bender. They could be completely innocent in all of this."

"We'll err on the side of caution," Chief Sheridan announces. He steps aside to get on his radio with his people and give them the rundown of what I've described.

Chief Perkins turns to me, releasing a heavy sigh. "Are you all right with this?" he asks. "You've been out here for hours. You must be exhausted."

I wish he wouldn't say that, since the last thing I need to think about is how many hours I've spent out here. Yes, I'm tired, but I'm also wired at the moment. No amount of caffeine leaves me this alert, this eager to get moving. I'm almost jumping out of my skin, my heart beating fast, my senses sharp.

"I'm just fine," I assure him. "When this is over, I plan on taking a vacation."

He doesn't know me nearly well enough to look as skeptical as he does. "You know what? I'm going to check up on you. I'm going to make sure you do that."

Once everything is in place, there's nothing to do but move in. "Please, give me one minute to try to get the baby out before you come in," I urge Chief Sheridan.

"We know how to handle these kinds of raids, Agent Forrest." I hold the man's gaze, refusing to blink until he does. "Of course. You'll have a minute. We'll be behind you."

I can't afford to take risks. Just because there's a baby present doesn't mean the woman I heard snap at Keaton is going to be in any mood to come along quietly. With that in mind, I check my pistol, making sure to leave my holster open under my jacket in case I need to go for it. All I can do is hope that won't be the case, for Isabel's sake.

A quick rap against the door does exactly what I knew it would. "Oh, come on!" a woman calls out a second after the baby starts to cry. "We just got her down! What is wrong with you?"

The door flies open, and the woman who opened it glares angrily at me before realizing we don't know each other. Instantly, her eyes narrow in suspicion and she backs up a step, glancing to her left where I'm guessing there's a weapon she suddenly wishes she could get her hands on.

I hold a finger up to my lips, shaking my head. "Wait a second," I urge in a whisper, knowing Sheridan and his people are behind me like he promised. "Nobody has to get hurt."

Keaton pops up on the second of two beds. Her face falls in dismay when she sees me. I don't acknowledge her, since doing so could get her in trouble. Besides, I'm a little too busy eyeing the woman in front of me. The woman who scoffs, looking me up and down. "Who do you think you are?"

"She's a cop," Keaton blurts out before scrambling from the bed. I really wish she hadn't said that.

"Freeze, where you are." I hate to draw my gun, but there's no choice. The woman in front of me goes still, lifting her hands into the air.

My gaze darts from her to a battered pack-and-play wedged between the beds. That's where crying is coming from. Keaton reaches inside for the baby, holds her close like a shield. I wish she hadn't done that, too.

"Nobody has to get hurt," I tell them again, while

footsteps ring out nearby, coming closer. "Just take it easy, stay calm, and we can all walk out of this." Meanwhile the baby shrieks, red faced, and I make the mistake of looking her way. Reflex, really. That's the only explanation.

"No!" Keaton cries out, and my attention swings back to the woman who is now reaching for a shotgun. Before she can grab hold I take her by the arm and shove her across the room, backing her up against the wall before officers move in. I hear them next door, as well, barking orders.

"Hand over the baby." One of Sheridan's men holds his arms out, coaxing Keaton.

Once her partner is secured, I do the same, approaching with caution. "Just let us have the baby," I murmur. "Like I told you, you're not in trouble. We only want to take the baby home, where she belongs. Look at her," I add, nodding toward the squalling infant. "She needs her mother, and her mother needs her. You did everything you could to take care of her."

Keaton's eyes fill with tears and her chin quivers, but she grudgingly hands Isabel over to me. Her diaper is wet and her onesie is soiled, but otherwise she seems all right.

"Hello, sweetheart," I whisper as I take off my jacket, passing her from one arm to the other so I can eventually wrap it around her. "It is so nice to meet you."

"Does she look all right?" Chief Perkins is waiting outside the room when I emerge. What started as a quiet, careful operation has now exploded into something much more tense and active, with men and women emerging from the rooms to either side of the one where Isabel was staying. They all look like they were woken out of a dead sleep, but the danger is clear once officers emerge with shotguns and ammunition. My eyes bulge as a seemingly endless arsenal is removed.

"Let's get her to a hospital," I announce, and Chief Sheridan leads the way to one of the unmarked cars which has now pulled into the lot.

"Take them over to Presbyterian, that's the closest," he tells the officer behind the wheel while I climb into the backseat with Isabel in my arms. The chief takes her for me while I buckle in, then hands her back. She's not crying anymore, but is still somewhat fussy, whimpering and fretting as I rest her against my shoulder.

"You're going to be okay," I tell her, rubbing her back, rocking her gently. "Everything's going to be all right now, sweetheart."

Even if we still haven't found her father. All I can do is hope that now, with these people in custody, we'll get some answers.

# 27

# Alexis

"But you're all right?" Naturally, that's Mitch's primary concern once I have finished giving him the rundown of what happened tonight.

"I'm just fine," I assure him. "Tired, but fine. Relieved more than anything."

Standing in the hall at the hospital, I take a deep breath and release it slowly, calming myself—or trying to. The hard part is over. Isabel is safe, currently being checked out by a team of doctors who up until now have declared dehydration her biggest problem. That, and a little diaper rash. "The baby is safe. I just wish I understood why they were keeping her there."

"Leverage," Mitch suggests before yawning. "Sorry. I'm riveted, trust me. But it's pretty late."

He's not kidding. The clock hanging on the wall at the nurses station reads 2:30. "I'm so sorry I woke you up. I thought I should let you know everything turned out as well as it could." Even if Ryan wasn't at the motel.

"I wasn't sleeping well, anyway. I sort of have this thing where I get a little bit of insomnia when I know my girlfriend is sneaking around shady characters, trying to stop the bad guys without getting herself hurt."

"I would tell you to go to sleep, but you only have to be up in a few hours, anyway."

"No, ma'am," he replies. "I have arranged coverage for myself. I plan on taking tomorrow off—and I think you should, too," he adds in a firm voice. "At the very least, you need a solid eight hours of sleep after everything you've done."

He's not wrong. It takes conscious effort just to move back and forth in front of the exam room, and I'm only doing that to keep myself alert. Jessica and Ethan should be on their way after the call telling them we have the baby. I want to be here when they arrive. But after that? Yes, sleep sounds like a wonderful idea.

There's just one problem. "I'm not sure I have it in me to drive all the way back. I'm afraid I would fall asleep on the road."

"I'll come to you. I'll pack a few of your things in a bag and I'll meet you. No arguments," he adds with a growl when I open my mouth to argue. "It's less than an hour drive, and I am much more alert than you sound. I'll be there in no time—there won't be any traffic at this time of night. We'll get a room someplace. Okay?"

"How about I get the room and let you know

where to meet me after Jessica gets here?" This seems to please him, so I promise to make a reservation—maybe at the hotel where Special Agent Childs' team is still staying as we work through the aftermath of the warehouse raid. There are so many moving pieces to this case, it's easy to lose track.

After making the call for a last-minute reservation, I'm surprised when Chief Perkins rounds the corner with a cup of coffee in each hand. "It's from one of those automatic machines," he explains, holding a cup out to me. "Figured you could use it."

I take it gratefully, and though my nose wrinkles—it smells a little burnt, even if it was just brewed —I swallow back a few gulps. "What brings you here? I figured you would be busy processing the people who were brought in."

"Not my jurisdiction, remember? Our departments are working together, since this ties in with the missing persons case, but it's up to Jim and his people to process the individuals who were arrested with that cache of weapons." He removes his hat, running a hand over his graying hair. "Enough for a small army. Makes you wonder what they were preparing for."

"I'm not sure we have to wonder," I muse, sipping more coffee, shaking my head. "I might not have been there long after the police started bringing people out, but I recognized two of the men after seeing them at the warehouse. I'm sure there are photos of them outside, standing guard."

"That sounds like good news to me." He lifts his

paper cup in my direction and I do the same. I'm sure we are both reflecting on how fortunate it was that everyone was asleep, unprepared for a bunch of armed officers to storm in and arrest them. Thinking back on the amount of firepower represented, it could have been a bloodbath.

"Well, Chief Sheridan has plenty of ammunition to use against these people," I point out, leaning against the wall for support. If it weren't for the chief being here, I might fall asleep. Jessica needs to arrive soon. "Hopefully he can get that motel closed down."

"That's tricky, though," he points out, scowling down at his coffee. "There are still plenty of people in the area who need a place to stay, someplace cheap where nobody asks questions. Not everybody there was in on this."

I see his point. "At the very least, here's hoping the owner starts paying attention and stops looking the other way. I don't know," I murmur, shaking my head and snickering at myself. "I'm probably naïve."

"I think you've seen way too much in your career to be considered naïve. That's all we can do in a situation like this, anyway. We can hope what we've done will make a difference to someone."

Something certainly made a difference. "Where is she? Where is my baby?" We both look down the hall, and a moment later Jessica comes running with Ethan behind her. "Izzy? Where is Izzy?" she demands, her face tearstained.

"In here. The doctors are finishing their exam." I can't imagine I would be happy to be stopped short the way I stop her, which is why I'm able to overlook her angry glare. "They're only getting finished now. Let them be sure she's all right, please. I carried her the whole way here, and she seemed healthy, but let's be sure."

A breathless sob escapes her before she covers her face with her hands. "I have to hold my baby. And where is my husband?" she demands, dropping her hands, looking back-and-forth between me and the chief. I'm sure my emotions would swing wildly if I were in her position.

"There were no signs of him at the motel," he informs her in a grave, respectful tone. "Half a dozen people were taken in for questioning."

"One of them is bound to give us answers," I tell her, doing everything I can to sound hopeful and positive though really, there are no guarantees. There never are. Every single one of them could plead ignorance or clam up entirely, refusing to speak unless their lawyer tells them it's safe. It happens all the time. That's the uncertain nature of this. We rely so much on the cooperation of others.

"Mom, he'll be okay." Ethan reaches up to put a hand on her shoulder. "Dad can take care of himself. But Izzy can't. She can come home now."

My heart goes out to him. I know all too well how it feels, trying to comfort your mother when you spent all your life being the one who is comforted. It's awkward, even painful.

She pats his hand, offering a shaky smile through her tears. "Of course, you're right. Your dad can handle whatever happens." There's strain in her voice, etched in the lines at the corners of her eyes. She looks like a woman who's been suffering sleepless nights.

"For what it's worth," I offer, "She seems strong and healthy."

"I just don't understand. Why would they have her? Why would he someplace like that? None of this makes any sense." I can see her biting her tongue, thinking twice about going any further while her son looks so interested in what she has to say—and so confused by it. I'm sure he's got a million questions, none of which are anywhere close to being answered.

The door to the exam room opens and a pair of doctors emerge. "Mrs. McAllister?" one of them asks. Jessica's head bobs, her eyes wide. Ethan grabs her hand. "You can go in and see her now. She seems just fine."

A sob bursts from her before she rushes into the room with Ethan at her side. I watch from the doorway as Jessica gathers Isabel up in her arms and holds her close, weeping over the baby's wispy hair. "Oh, sweetheart, oh, Mommy missed you so much. My sweet baby."

Ethan wraps his arms around her waist and buries his face in her side, and she puts an arm around him while continuing to weep over Isabel. I have to blink tears away before stepping back into the hall to give them their privacy.

It's a bittersweet reunion—at least, it feels bittersweet to me. "We're not finished," I whisper more to

myself than to the chief, but he grunts his understanding.

"We're getting there. Get half a dozen people in
interrogation rooms and pit them against each other,
and you see how quickly the whole operation comes
tumbling down. All it takes is putting pressure on the
right person. We're going to find him," he concludes
with a firm nod.

"I know," I sigh.

"Right now, we're going to take this win and be
happy for it. And we are both going to get some
sleep," he adds, narrowing his eyes at me. "There's no
coming out on the other side of this successfully if
everybody is sleep deprived."

"Right you are." I sketch a quick salute and offer a
weary smile. "My boyfriend is bringing a bag out here
for me so I don't have to drive all the way home. I got
us a room nearby." I could weep as a thought. My
whole body cries out for the luxury of a bed. That's all
I want. A simple bed, a pillow, maybe a blanket if
somebody's feeling generous, but I won't be picky.

"I'm glad to hear it. I can drive you over there, if
you want," he offers, and now I remember I left my
car parked by the adult store. The idea of going back
to get it is unthinkable. I'm too exhausted. I'll have
Mitch drive me back there in the morning. At this
rate, though, it won't be until afternoon. I can't
imagine waking up early once my head hits the pillow.

After saying our goodbyes to Jessica and promising
to check in with her later, we leave the hospital and
step out into the chilly, peaceful night. Strange. It

wasn't so peaceful earlier. Beyond the hospital there are homes full of people fast asleep. I almost envy their ignorance sometimes.

But inside the hospital, in an exam room is a very happy mother and a little boy who got his baby sister back. The chief is right. We have to take the win.

# 28

# Alexis

It's early afternoon by the time I arrive at the station, where Chief Sheridan is holding the people we brought in last night. I can't pretend a solid eight hours of sleep didn't help. I feel like a new woman after picking up my car, waiting for me outside the windowless building where I left it last night. Mitch didn't bother pretending the whole thing wasn't funny.

"Alexis Forrest." He clicked his tongue, shaking his head. "I would never have expected it from you."

"Hey, for all you know, I was picking up a few tips and tricks to bring home." We were both laughing as we parted ways. I get the feeling he was just happy to spend time together after my stakeout and subsequent raid.

It's easier to be in a good mood, feeling focused and hopeful now that I've rested. Chief Sheridan waves me into his office, where he jumps straight into a rundown of everything I've missed. "We're having a heckuva time trying to get any of them to talk," he reports, grimacing. "Can't tell if they're afraid of retribution, or if they just don't feel like cooperating."

I can't say I'm surprised. The woman I faced off with last night, staying in the room with Keaton, was ready to pull a shotgun on me and would have if given the opportunity. "I guess that means nobody has said a word about Ryan McAllister."

"As far as they're concerned, there is no one named Ryan McAllister." I can't tell if he sounds aggravated over the story he's sharing, or the fact that all of the paper cups on his desk are empty. He looks into the last of them, scowling before tossing it in the trash. "For all we know, that could be true as far as they're concerned. He might not have used his name."

"Keaton knew his name, at least his first name," I remind him. "Where is she?"

"In one of the holding cells just like the others. She's the only one who's been remotely cooperative so far, but the way she tells it, she hasn't been a part of things for very long. Boyfriend of hers was involved with the group and that's how she got roped in. Now, the boyfriend's history, and she doesn't feel like she can get out. She knows too much."

I can't imagine having to live this way. Trapped like that, nowhere to go. She feels friendless and abandoned. "Maybe this can be a way out for her," I suggest, though she isn't really my main concern.

And of course, the chief knows that. "You're more than welcome to go down there and start asking questions, see if anybody is more willing to open up to you.

Agents Morgan and DeMeo are already here, waiting on you."

He could've told me that already. Childs must have reassigned them, asked them to come in and help out. We meet up outside one of the interrogation rooms and formulate a plan. "We'll split up," I decide, "and handle the women first. There's four of them, two men. Keaton claims she doesn't have much information to share—let's focus on the other three, instead."

I know who I want to talk to. The woman from Keaton's room. Her name is Angela, and according to her records she's twenty-three years old. She could pass for someone in her mid-thirties, at least, but a lot of that probably has to do with the confrontational glare she gives me when I enter the room, the way her shoulders rise up around her ears.

"I know you," she tells me before I have a chance to say a word, then rattles the cuff and chain attaching her wrist to the table. Her eyes narrow. "Why do I need this?"

"Why do you think?" I counter, taking a seat across from her. "You attempted to pull a firearm on a federal agent last night. We tend to treat that sort of thing seriously."

"I wasn't anywhere close to reaching it."

"Well, we can't afford to rely on technicalities." Folding my hands on the table, I wait until she meets my gaze before saying another word. "I understand you weren't interested in speaking much."

"That's right." Her thin lips tighten in an even

thinner line chock full of contempt. "I have nothing to say."

"Are you sure about that?" I ask, maintaining a low and neutral tone. "You were shacked up in that motel. Taking care of a baby that's not yours. There was a firearm in that room, and many more in the rooms to either side of the one you were in. From what I see here," I continue, flipping through her file, "you've already been picked up over a handful of offenses. You must know it will go better for you if you cooperate."

"I don't need to cooperate, because I didn't do anything."

"Are you sure your friends are going to corroborate that story? Or will they point the finger at you when their time comes to be questioned?" She narrows her dark eyes again, skeptical, on alert. Wondering if I'm telling the truth or if this is a means of tricking her into saying more than she should.

"Listen." She takes a deep breath, then releases it slowly. "I mean it. I don't know anything. What, you think they were giving us details? We're women." Disdain drips from the word as she rolls her eyes.

"That's the prevailing attitude?" I shake my head, clicking my tongue. "I can't say I'm surprised."

This is good. This could mean the difference between her opening up and continuing to stonewall me. "So, what? You hang around all day waiting for them to tell you what to do? Is that how it goes? You can tell me without incriminating yourself," I assure her. "I'm just trying to get an idea of why you girls were there if you're not active members of this enterprise."

"Enterprise." She blows out a soft whistle. "Don't let any of the guys hear that. They'll start getting big ideas about themselves."

Somehow, that doesn't surprise me, either. "But it is a big enterprise," I point out. "I'm sure you know we arrested a handful of the people involved, down at one of the warehouses the group uses to process shipments. They're currently cooling their heels in jail, awaiting trial. It's not looking good for them."

Her tongue darts over her lips before she clears her throat. "I don't know what you want from me."

"I think you know exactly what I want from you, Angela." My tone is firmer now. It's time to stop playing games. "Let's start with you not insulting my intelligence by expecting me to believe you don't know anything about what goes on. We know after conducting surveillance there was at least one instance in which a man arrived at the motel and left with a bag he wasn't carrying when he showed up. We have records of several instances like that, people coming and going. I was approached by someone who tried to run me off, so there wouldn't be any trouble from the authorities. And at the end of the day," I conclude, "you were looking after a baby who was kidnapped. The subject of an ongoing investigation. It doesn't look good for you, especially when you continue to stonewall."

She wants to stare me down. To frustrate me to the point where I give up. I can see through her—she's wounded, she's been through a lot. She's seen more than she should have at her age.

And at the end of the day, she's afraid. When I shift my perspective and look at her that way, it's easier to feel patience and compassion. "Angela," I softly implore, "you're not helping yourself by protecting any of these people. We can help you."

Scoffing, she sits back in the chair while her mouth twists into a smirk. Tucking a strand of sandy blond hair behind one ear, she mutters, "Nice words. Anybody can promise anything if it gets them what they want. That doesn't mean I have to believe you."

"All I ask is that you give us a direction to go in," I counter, thinking fast, trying to stay ahead of her. "That baby's father is still missing. Even if you don't know specifics, you must know the name of someone who does."

Her jaw works. Her nostrils flare. When her chin starts to quiver, I know I've got her. " Maybe … " Her teeth sink into her lip, her gaze landing on the table and staying there. "Maybe you could find something back at the motel. Maybe there's something hidden there, in one of the rooms you jerks busted into. But what do I know?" she concludes with a shrug.

"Thank you," I whisper. She shrugs again, refusing to look at me as I stand.

The motel. Something is hidden at the motel. "I want back up!" I bark on my way down the hall, past Sheridan's open door. "There's information at the motel. We need to find it."

Within ten minutes, we are back at the scene of

the crime. The three rooms we entered last night are taped off, guarded by a small group of local PD who step aside at the sight of my badge. It only takes a moment for me to give them the rundown. "We're looking for hidden documents, files, whatever. I don't have specifics," I admit, "but let's keep an eye out for hidden compartments in the walls, in the floors, anything."

Looking toward the front office, I add, "Something tells me we're not going to get any help from management."

"She's pleading ignorance," one of the officers tells me, and it comes as no surprise.

We split up, checking all three rooms at once. We move beds to the side, shift furniture to check for panels in the walls that could be removed. "Do yourself a favor and don't look in the ceiling," someone calls out from one of the adjacent rooms, coughing. "Unless you're wearing a mask."

I glance up at the tiles above my head and decide to forgo that unless there's no other option. If Angela knew about it, that tells me whatever she's talking about was probably in her room, the one I'm examining. The one in which a pack and play still sits, the bottom covered in ratty blankets.

"Agent Forrest? Check this out." One of the officers with me waves me into the bathroom, where they've dislodged a panel in the wall under the sink. "I assumed it was access to the pipes at first."

It's not. "Have the others check the bathrooms for this," I tell him, pulling on gloves before reaching inside and withdrawing a stack of folders, books, and papers wrapped in a plastic bag.

The first book I pull from inside the bag is a ledger like the one I found at Ryan's house. There are maps, flash drives. It's going to take hours upon hours to go through all of it.

I can hardly wait.

## 29

## Alexis

"Have I told you lately how glad I am you're here?"

Agent DeMeo's dark eyes crinkle at the corners but don't drift from the screen in front of him. He is serious, driven, which I can certainly appreciate. "I'm just glad for an opportunity to get out of the office."

With a wry smirk, he glances around the room in which we've set up our base of operations at the police station. "I mean, I'm in another office, but at least it's a change of scene."

I might be micromanaging, hanging around like this, waiting for … What? A miracle? When the alternative is leaving without getting a look at whatever he finds, the choice is clear.

Still, I make it a point to check the time as discreetly as possible. He's been attempting to decrypt the information on the flash drives for the past ninety minutes. I know these things don't happen in the blink of an eye, but is it too much to wish they would?

Rather than drive him crazy by hanging over his

shoulder, I turn my attention to the ledger books. Like the ones I found before, they are coded, filled with initials. FR. LH. JM. They could stand for names, of course, but they could also stand for literally anything else. I have no way of decoding any of this, and I know if we were to ask any of the people we brought in from the motel, I would get nothing but blank stares.

"It seems a little risky."

I look over toward agent DeMeo. "What does?" I ask, though of course there are any number of things he could be referring to. This whole situation is risky, which I'm sure is no secret to the people involved. Yet somehow, they're still part of it. I have to remind myself of what Keaton told the officers when she was questioned. She's trapped. I wonder how many of the individuals involved in all of this are going through the same thing. Even the men.

"Leaving things lying around. Yes, they were hidden," he adds with a shrug. "But not very well. At the end of the day, this still seems very slapdash, and yet they use sophisticated encryption."

"I'll tell you. I stopped trying to figure out a lot of things a long time ago," I admit. "Recently, my boyfriend and I were wondering about what these people could do if they took their intelligence and used it for good."

"You mean legally?" he suggests, and we share a brief smile. "I know. Then again, they keep us employed, right?" A rather grim observation, but he makes a point.

There's a brief knock at the door, and I open it to find Agent Morgan on the other side. "Just wanted to let you know Keaton Wright was released. Claims she has family in Bangor. One of Chief Sheridan's deputies is driving her to her parents' house."

I'm glad to hear it. Hopefully, this will be the start of something better for her. "Here's hoping she stays away from guys like her ex," I muse.

The agent shakes his head, snorting like I said something funny. "I think we both know the odds of that are pretty low."

He's probably right, but if I didn't at least try to hope for better, I wouldn't be able to do this job. What's the point of getting the bad guys off the streets if we can't hope for better in the future?

It's funny, the way my phone rings just as I'm thinking about Keaton and her bad luck with men. The man calling me is a living, breathing example of good luck. Maybe the best luck of my entire life. I step out of the room to give DeMeo space and grab myself a measure of privacy before answering. "How did you know I was thinking about you?" I ask Mitch with a smile.

"Here's hoping it was for a good reason and not because you decided to run away with the owner of that bookstore."

"You are really going to have to let that go," I murmur, chuckling.

He chuckles with me. "Just hoping to get a little laugh from you. How's it going?"

"Slowly," I tell him, groaning softly. "I'm worried.

Obviously, whoever has Ryan knows by now about the raid. There's a chance they could get rid of him just to keep him quiet, trying to mitigate the damage."

"You probably know what I'm going to tell you."

"Maybe I need to hear it, anyway," I point out, leaning my back against the wall, keeping my voice low for the sake of privacy as officers travel the hallway. I doubt any of them are paying attention, but still.

"If they did ... dispatch with him," he ventures, "that is not your fault. You didn't make any of this happen."

I know he means it. I even know he's right. Somehow, that doesn't quite loosen the growing tension between my shoulder blades, running up my neck, filling my head. "There must be something I've missed."

"Something all of you missed," he insists gently, but firmly. He is not in the mood to argue about this. "Where did you get the idea you are the only person responsible for any of this?"

"I am the agent who was first assigned to the case, don't forget. I'm heading this whole thing up. So yes, it is sort of my responsibility." I love him for wanting to make me feel better, I do, but there are times when his aggressive positivity falls flat. It doesn't matter how many times I tell myself I'm not responsible. There's a reason every case has its lead agent. I can't ignore that.

"All right, but still. You are not the only person working it. You have given so much of yourself to this case, to every case. You need to get used to the idea."

"What idea?" I ask with a sigh.

"The idea of stepping back and letting other people be responsible every once in a while. Knowing you did everything you could, you gave your people all the information. You sat out there in the middle of nowhere, while I waited here at home with my heart in my throat, conducting surveillance when the Bureau wouldn't provide backup or a team to work in shifts. Thanks to that, you have people in custody, you have all of that information you found at the motel. And," he concludes with something like smugness in his tone, "Isabel is home with her mother. If that's not going above and beyond, I don't know what is."

I have to smile, and it's not surprising when the tension knotting my muscles up dissolves. Not entirely, not all at once, but it starts to thanks in large part to Mitch's uncanny ability to put things in perspective when I lose sight of the big picture. Yet another reason why I need him in my life.

"Thank you." It comes out as a grateful whisper. "Maybe I should bring you around with me wherever I go. It could be your job. Calming me down, reminding me of the important things when I forget."

"An interesting proposal. What does the benefits package look like?"

"We can't offer much in the way of a retirement plan," I admit, "but you can get all the hugs and kisses you want."

"I might have to weigh my options. I mean, the hugs and kisses part sounds great," he allows, "but I can't pay the mortgage with hugs and kisses. Believe me, if you saw my banker, you would understand why I don't want to."

It is entirely too easy to lose sight of real life sometimes. Easy to develop tunnel vision. Laughing with him reconnects me. "I'll take your concerns back to management and see if we can work something out."

"Will you be home tonight?"

It occurs to me there's nothing I want more. "Definitely. I doubt we're going to make a ton of progress today, anyway." And it's already almost dinner time. Still no answers.

At least, that's what I think when I end the call. Once I check in with agent DeMeo, however, I am met with a pleasant surprise. "Look what I found." He pushes back from the desk in his wheeled chair, arms folded, grinning with pride.

"You decrypted it?"

"Roughly half of what was contained in the drives, yes."

I have to pull up a chair of my own before I start poring over the information. "GPS coordinates," I murmur, spotting three, four, five instances of them. "Locations."

"I'm already making note of them," he tells me as I continue going through what he unlocked. There's so much here.

"It's going to take ages to get through all of this," I murmur, my heart sinking. "Like trying to drink from a fire hose." And right away, there's guilt because I just told Mitch I'd be home tonight.

"Well, that's why there's an entire team of us

working on this." He removes his glasses and cleans them on his polo shirt. "I know if I spend another hour looking at a screen, my eyes will cross, and I might have to run screaming up and down the hall. Everyone has their limits." He's right, just like he's right that there are others to work on this.

"I'll forward all of this to Special Agent Childs," I decide. It feels like the right thing to do, even if I'd rather go through it on my own. But DeMeo has a point. I don't know long I'd be able to claw my way through it without going a little nutty. "He can assign techs to parse the information, identify patterns."

"That sounds like a very good idea. Tomorrow, we'll be able to hit the ground running."

I only wish I didn't feel this nagging regret as I give Childs a call to let him know what's coming his way.

# 30

# Alexis

"Well, we know the information in those files wasn't fabricated to throw us off their tracks." My eyes are glued to what I see in front of me thanks to my binoculars. We are roughly half a mile back from the waterfront, where a series of docks line a seldom-used wharf.

"This used to be a pretty busy place," Agent Morgan muses from the passenger seat of the unmarked car we're using for surveillance purposes. "Lots of boats in and out. Then they built that big harbor further up the coast and diverted the shipping over there. Plenty of guys lost their jobs."

When I look his way, lowering the binoculars, he chuckles. "Yeah, my dad was one of them. My uncles, too. It was a long time ago, when I was a kid."

"I'm sorry. That must've been tough." I can hardly imagine this nearly abandoned area bustling with people and business. I've spotted three different stray dogs weaving in and out of tall grass, but what this area seems to specialize in is litter. It's become a dumping ground of sorts—there are trash bags, fast food containers, even an old mattress stained with ... I don't want to think about it. And over all of it, present all the time, is the nose-wrinkling aroma coming from the water. It's low tide, meaning the smell is especially pungent.

All of that fades into the background, present but unimportant thanks to the series of what are now nothing more than weatherbeaten shacks lining the wharf. I'm sure in better times, they held the goods coming in and going out. Now, they're probably home to even more stray animals and maybe the occasional vagrant seeking shelter from the elements. I have to wonder how much shelter they could find there, though, considering the condition of some of the roofs and windows from where we are parked.

I also have to wonder whether outsiders would be allowed to trespass, since the presence of half a dozen cars and armed guards would probably dissuade them.

"There. There he is." I'm surprised the sound of my rapid heartbeat isn't audible throughout the car once Viper comes into view. I would know him anywhere. The man's face has been etched in my memory ever since that night at the warehouse, when he barely escaped. "When he ran like the coward he is," I whisper.

"What's that?" Agent Morgan asks. I hadn't realized I'd said it out loud.

"I was only thinking about the last time I saw him," I explain, watching him light up a cigarette while clearly irritated with the men around him. He gestures a lot with the hand holding the cigarette, at one point bringing the glowing tip within inches of a man's face.

"What do you think it would be like, working for somebody like that?" Agent Morgan asks before blowing out a sigh. "I mean, Childs has been known to reduce grown men to something close to tears when he puts his mind to it, but watching this? I'm almost compelled to thank him for his patience."

I would laugh, but I'm busy watching every move Viper makes. "He is the key to all of this," I murmur, my eyes glued. "We can't let him go this time."

"We won't," he promises. "We'll have more cars, more bodies, boats in the water in case he tries to escape that way." Using the laptop mounted to the dash, he pulls up some of the decrypted information DeMeo uncovered yesterday. "If our theories are correct, their meeting is scheduled to start in half an hour. And I just got confirmation from DeMeo that half of Chief Perkins' department is coming out to participate."

I wish they would hurry. "Do you think the visitor referenced in those communications is Ryan McAllister?" I've been asking myself that question all day, ever since I reviewed the messages from one of the flash drives. When I get my hands on Viper and have a chance to sit down in an interrogation room, I can't wait to ask what the purpose of those drives is. Blackmail? A way to keep everybody in line? Otherwise, why would they keep these messages they've exchanged? Why would they hold them in a separate location, hidden from view?

"Even if it isn't," he reasons, "someone is. They're holding someone in one of those buildings." And according to some of the messages, he is becoming a liability. *The visitor is more trouble than he's worth. The visitor has brought other visitors around, looking for him. Maybe it would be better if he visited someplace else.*

I don't want to imagine them hinting at killing him—but at the same time, I have to wonder why they've kept him alive this long, if it is indeed Ryan McAllister being held captive. All the more reason to make sure Viper doesn't get away this time.

The sun has set by the time we get word all units are in place. I'm impressed—I didn't notice any activity in the vicinity, yet there are eight cars now forming a three-sided perimeter around the shoreline, with boats less than a mile out to watch for any traffic on the water. Just in time, too—there's heightened activity, a small caravan of pickup trucks rolling in. We take note of the seven men who enter one of the shacks, the largest of all, the one in the best condition. There are lights glowing behind broken windows.

When I give the command, we approach with caution, all of us driving in with our headlights off, going slowly—torturously slow as far as I'm concerned, but it's the only way. We're no more than a few hundred yards from the wharf when we come to a stop.

"I want one officer to hang back at each vehicle," I remind everyone listening on the radio. "Keep watch for anyone who tries to flee. The tall one in the black coat is our top priority. We want him brought in alive."

"Alexis." Agent Morgan nudges me, pointing through the windshield. It's Viper, and the way he's stopped still after stepping out with his phone in hand tells me he senses something is wrong. He would. Those instincts of his are all that's kept him in one piece this long.

"Wait," I whisper into the radio, my heart in my throat. What's he going to do? Is he going to run again? This time, we can chase him in our vehicles rather than trying to catch him on foot, which gives us an advantage. "If he goes for one of the vehicles, we're going in."

I've barely gotten the sentence out of my mouth when he does exactly what I predicted, jogging toward the closest sedan. "Go, go, go," I bark out before hurling myself from the car, my pistol in hand, my sights set on him. He is not getting away from me this time.

He spots us coming for him, some on foot, some behind the wheel as a flood of bright headlights paints the shack's walls and reveals the cold, hate-filled snarl he's wearing.

It takes him a few seconds of looking around to decide his best bet is going back inside, where there are others to do the fighting for him. I hear them in there, their voices somehow louder than the pounding of my heart.

Within moments, the high-pitched whine of bullets pierce the air dangerously close to my ear.

I take cover behind one of the pickup trucks and return fire through the closest broken window. A deep groan rings out inside the shack, and I take the opportunity to run for the door Viper disappeared through while others engage in a firefight. One of Chief Perkins' officers falls to the ground, eyes open and staring at the sky, and I almost stop before reminding myself who's waiting inside. Not this time. I am not leaving here without him.

"Forrest!" I catch sight of Agent Morgan sprinting toward me, and he serves as my cover once we enter what's clearly being used as a warehouse, probably a backup after we raided and emptied another. Men hide behind rows of crates and we do the same, returning fire, moving deeper into the space that now reeks of gunpowder, blood.

"Viper!" I shout when I spot his black coat before he disappears around the corner.

I cannot let him go. I won't. All I can do is pray I'm not making a huge mistake as I take off after him, hoping speed will help me avoid getting hit. One of the crates above my head bursts open in a rain of splinters and wood shards but I only duck, arms crossed over my head, running flat-out for the front of the building.

He's near the wide, open door leading out to the docks. "Viper!" I bark. He doesn't stop until I fire a warning shot over his head, the bullet lodging in a wooden beam. He flinches, ducking the way I did moments ago.

"Drop your weapon!" I shout, planting my feet at shoulder width, aiming for his leg to keep from firing a fatal shot. "There are boats out there waiting for you. We're surrounded. You are not getting away this time."

"Yeah?" He turns to me, meets my gaze, and a chill runs through my body. I am looking at an evil man, someone devoid of kindness or pity, someone who truly does not believe he'll ever be stopped. He's even smiling.

I soon figure out why when his gaze shifts over my shoulder and I realize I'm a sitting duck.

A gunshot rings out and for one heartstopping moment, I know this is it. I finally took one chance too many, acted before thinking, let the moment get away from me.

"Freeze right there!" I realize it's Agent Morgan shouting, that he shot whoever was about to take a shot at me. He's now backing me up, holding his weapon on Viper the way I am. "End of the line, Viper. Drop your weapon and you don't have to get hurt."

The man stands stock still, a semi automatic still clutched in his right hand. I force myself to breathe, waiting, wondering. Hoping.

When his mouth quirks up at one corner, I know he's made up his mind, and my finger squeezes the trigger before he has the chance to aim at either of us.

A shot to his kneecap won't kill him, but it does take him down while making him howl in pain.

Agent Morgan quickly disarms him while I approach, fighting to catch my breath. There are so many things I need to know, but one question rings out above the others. "Where is Ryan McAllister? Tell us, and this doesn't have to be so hard for you."

Even through his pain, he smiles, meeting my gaze in a defiant glare. "Don't worry. He's still breathing," he grunts, his teeth gritted. "But until I get a deal, you'll never know where to find him."

# 31

## Alexis

"This feels kind of silly."

Dr. Gretchen Meyer tips her head to the side, offering a gentle smile. It's a practiced expression, one I myself have worn for years. Friendly, warm, encouraging, but offering nothing concrete. "Silly? What do you mean?"

My gaze travels over her office—warm, cozy, arranged carefully. "I mean, I can't help but look around here and see it through a psychiatrist's eyes."

"Because of your training."

Nodding slowly, I chuckle at myself. "It's not easy for me to sit here as a patient when I already know everything that must be going on in your head when you look at me."

Her eyes narrow slightly. "What do you mean by that? Why do you think you know what's going on in my head?"

That came out wrong. I shift in the chair, trying and failing to ignore the sense of a spotlight shining directly on me, leaving me nowhere to hide. "I'm sure it's not easy for anybody with their PhD to then turn around and sit in therapy."

"That is a very interesting assertion." She folds her hands in her lap, the image of professionalism in a modest sheath dress and cardigan sweater. "Let's look a little more at that. What makes you think doctors would find it challenging to be in treatment? If anything, people in our profession understand the importance of having someone to talk to, someone to help them sort through their own personal life so they can in turn help others. I mean, I would be a hypocrite if I scoffed at the idea of sharing my thoughts and feelings with a trusted therapist—which I do," she adds, lifting a shoulder.

Could I blush harder than I already am? Could I feel much smaller? "Of course. I don't know what I'm saying."

"Do you often backpedal so suddenly?" she asks. "Do you find it difficult to back up your assertions?"

And this is exactly why I didn't want to see the therapist Mitch so strongly urged me to see. She works within the Bureau, specializing in treating agents after traumatic experiences on the job. An absolutely necessary role, putting it mildly.

Yet somehow, I have a hard time imagining myself benefiting from her help. Why? "Do this for me," Mitch begged when I balked at the suggestion. "And for yourself. You can't spend the rest of your life trying to make up for what happened when you were a kid.

You couldn't control it then, and there's nothing you can really do about it now."

She asked a question, didn't she? "It's funny," I admit, "but I never saw it that way before. Back peddling. I guess I do that sometimes."

"Can you identify any triggers?"

I know exactly what she's getting it, and it almost makes me grind my teeth when I see everything laid out in front of me. No doubt I'm easy to read—that shouldn't irritate me, but it does. "I'm sure you can see in my file that my sister was murdered when I was ten years old."

She nods slowly, her brows drawing together in an expression of sympathy. "Yes, I did read that. I'm so sorry you went through such a traumatic event."

"So, putting two and two together? I developed this habit when I was trying to survive. Whenever I said something that didn't land the right way, I had to take it back."

"Can you think of any examples? I'm trying to understand." She crosses her legs, leaning forward slightly.

"You know. Simple things, like asking if we could have pizza for dinner. Or whether I could ride my bike on a Saturday morning. I always had to watch to judge the reaction. I didn't want to upset the apple cart. Mom already had enough to worry about."

"I see. I find that is a common tactic employed by people who grew up in traumatic or uncertain circumstances. The certainty that they are responsible for the feelings and reactions of those around them. It's a way for them to protect others—and themselves," she adds with a note of sympathy in her voice. "Does that resonate with you?"

"You know, it does," I admit, reaching for the bottle of water she offered when I arrived. It doesn't do much to clear the lump in my throat. "I'm sorry. I'm not trying to be confrontational or difficult. I am in the middle of a case, and we made a big breakthrough last night."

"And you would rather be working. I understand. But sometimes, we have to go through uncomfortable things in the present so we can function better in the future. The case will still be there," she reminds me, tucking her bobbed brown hair behind her ear. "And when the case is over, what happens to you? That's why we're here."

In other words, she is not letting me off the hook. Settling back in the chair, I fold my hands the way she's folded hers. "What can I do? I know I have a lot to work on, and it isn't like I enjoy feeling so much … " I can't find the word. It gets stuck in my throat. The way the doctor waits with her eyebrows raised isn't helping.

Finally, she prompts, "Pressure?" When my head bobs, she sighs. "Again, I have no doubt you are stuck in those old patterns from when you were a kid. And that's all it is, getting stuck. You can get unstuck. I've seen it happen, but it takes work. Conscious effort. Learning to identify them in the moment, then flipping the script. That's the only way through, the only hope of lasting change. Do you think you can do that?"

"I don't think I have a choice." My throat closes up right at the moment I feel the most vulnerable, making me choke a little on my words.

"Take your time, Alexis," she murmurs. She's still not letting me off the hook. I have no choice but to express my thoughts, no matter how I would like to ignore them or push them aside.

"I guess while we're talking in terms of triggers," I murmur after sipping from the water bottle, "my entire career is one big trigger."

"Let's talk a little more about that. What compelled you to pursue this career?"

I have to laugh, holding up a hand while I do. "I'm sorry. I'm not trying to insult you. But I think the answer is pretty obvious."

"It's not my job to draw conclusions. That's your job."

Whew. She's tough. I like her for it. "Fair enough. I'm doing this because I know how it feels, too. Praying for answers. Praying somebody can help, then sitting back and waiting for it to happen. The helplessness. I want to take that feeling away from victims and their families. I hate the thought of anybody going through what we went through."

She takes her time, letting it sink in before murmuring, "That is admirable. When do you step back and remind yourself you aren't responsible for what these people are going through?"

"I don't consider myself responsible for that, but I am responsible for getting justice."

"That is an awful lot of responsibility. It must be exhausting."

I understand she's trying to draw me out of my shell, guiding me toward the revelations that must seem so obvious to her. She has that luxury. She can sit and look in from the outside. "I'm afraid it's more exhausting for the people who care about me. Like my boyfriend."

"There you go again. Worrying about others, brushing your needs aside the way you backpedaled to protect the adults around you." Before I can respond, she asks, "How does he figure into this?"

"I'm here because he begged me to make the appointment," I admitted, making her chuckle. "Beyond that, he appreciates my dedication–but only in as much as it doesn't jeopardize my life."

"He sounds like a caring boyfriend."

"Yes, and I know I can only hurt him by not getting a handle on myself. I know it's not fair to him when I take risks. Frankly, I'm not used to having to consider somebody else. It's only a recent development, rebuilding a relationship with my parents, and aside from Mitch, I haven't had a long-term, steady romantic relationship in years. Nothing with a future."

"But you think you have a future with Mitch?" she asks with a smile.

That, I don't need to think about. "He is my future. He is my past. He's my constant."

The snapping of her fingers tells me I hit paydirt.

"And that, right there, tells me you are going to find a way to process your past and learn to let it influence, but not rule, the present. You have no idea how many people I see who can't identify a reason to keep working on themselves. The people who think they are a completely lost cause."

"I don't think I'm a lost cause." That much, I don't have to think about. "If anything, most of the time I wish the people around me would try to see things through my eyes the way I try to see things through theirs."

She nods slowly. "The coping mechanisms you developed as a child are just that, the coping mechanisms of a child. They worked for you then, the way you needed them to, but it's time to develop new mechanisms for the present day. That means no longer taking responsibility for the actions of others, the reactions of others. You're a deeply empathetic person and I'm sure that informs your work and makes you an excellent agent, but as with all things in life, it's crucial that you learn to set boundaries."

I have to laugh. "That has never been one of my talents."

"So I suspected." She draws a deep breath and lets it out slowly. "That's what we're here for. But this is more than a one-and-done situation. We're not going to unlock all the answers today, in a single session. I would like to help you, really, but I need to know you are going to work consistently on this with me. Will you? If I have your word, we can schedule a series of sessions together and take it one step at a time. What do you think about that?"

*Please, do this for me. I can't stand watching you torture yourself the way you do.* Mitch's pained expression is fresh in my memory—it was what finally broke through my stubbornness and convinced me to show up here today. Even if I don't want to do this for myself, I want to do it for him. For us. "If you can help me figure out how to make sense of everything I'm carrying around in me, by all means. I know I found a good thing. I want to protect it."

She offers a satisfied smile. "I'm glad to hear it. Let's get to work, Alexis."

# 32

# Alexis

I wish I could say I feel like a new woman by the time I enter the hospital, where the near frenzy of activity doesn't do much to mask the sense of deep sorrow hanging over the officers milling around the ICU. Neil Pierce was a fifteen-year veteran of the department before being killed last night during the raid on the wharf.

Officers have placed strips of black electrical tape over their badges, a sign of mourning for their lost colleague. My heart goes out to all of them, but especially to the man's family. I wonder if his wife and kids ever sat up worrying the way Mitch worries about me. I'm sure in a small and generally quiet town like this, they weren't normally too concerned. Here we are today, with one officer deceased and two more in the hospital after sustaining gunshots.

"Ramirez and Danvers are still critical, but they're strong. They'll pull through." Chief Perkins' sorrow is palpable as he gives me the rundown on what I've missed.

"I'm sorry I'm only coming in now," I offer, checking the time and wincing. "I had an appointment I couldn't miss this morning."

He tips his head to the side, brows knitting together. "You don't work for me, remember? You don't have to report your schedule. Besides, I know you wouldn't be gone for long," he adds with a chuckle that does nothing for the flat grief in his eyes. "Everything all right?"

"Oh, just fine." Granted, I have weekly visits with Dr. Meyer to look forward to, but it helped a little when she reminded me she has weekly appointments of her own with a doctor.

"Because we're professionals doesn't mean we're beyond the need for help," she reminded me before I left her office. "If anything, it should be easier for us, knowing what we know. There are all sorts of reasons why a person needs someone to talk to. Someone to help sift through the noise of daily life. It's not a sign of weakness. It's strength."

Why in the world do I have such a hard time accepting that? I know she's right—and I would offer the exact same advice to anyone who came to me. Why am I exempt from that? Why can I not give myself the same grace I would give a total stranger?

Now is not the time to worry about that. I can't say I'm sweeping it under the rug, either, since I do have a series of follow-up sessions scheduled. The presence of Viper, currently handcuffed to a bed after surgery on his kneecap, is what deserves the bulk of my attention today. I haven't worked tirelessly to bring him in only to drop the ball now.

"He's under twenty-four hour surveillance," the chief assures me on the way to Viper's room at the end of the hall. "We are taking zero chances."

Which is precisely why he's being held in the ICU, to allow for heightened attention from the staff and law enforcement officers. "I'm glad to hear that." We arrive at the room, where a glass wall eliminates the possibility of the patient pulling a fast one, so to speak. There is nothing he can hide. No secret visits, nothing that could pose a threat to anyone in the hospital.

I won't bother pretending it isn't gratifying, seeing him reduced to this. Helpless, currently immobile thanks to the shot I fired. His eyes are closed now, but he's not sleeping. I feel it. He's an animal pondering its next move. Plotting. Not that it's going to make much of a difference, but whatever he needs to cling to to get him through.

All at once, his eyes snap open. The same cold, empty eyes I looked into last night. Dark eyes which now turn my way, his head rotating on the pillow so his gaze can lock with mine. Is that the beginnings of a smirk forming at the corners of his mouth? Like we're in on a joke the rest of the world isn't privy to.

I wonder how many times this monster has been given a dose of his own medicine. This has to be unusual for him.

Rather than stand around staring, I make the choice of entering his room without announcing my intentions to Chief Perkins, who follows silently in my wake. Viper arches an eyebrow but says nothing, watching with that same strange sense of amusement. "How's the knee?" I ask, stepping up to the foot of his bed, eyeing the mass of bandages around the affected area.

"It's been better." Now he smirks full-on, his eyes crinkling at the corners. "No thanks to you."

"I was doing my job."

"The way I do mine."

"Not exactly," I fire back. He is not going to draw a parallel between us. I'm willing to give him enough rope to hang himself with, but some things I cannot allow. "I don't profit from the pain of others, the way you do."

"Whatever you need to tell yourself, Agent … What is it again?" he asks, frowning. "Woods?"

Cute. I'm sure he amuses himself. "Forrest. Agent Forrest."

"Close enough," he says with a sigh, wincing as he moves slightly on the bed. His jaw works, nostrils flaring, but he tries to play it off. "I'll have to remember that every time my knee twinges for the rest of my life."

"I'm glad to know you'll never forget me."

He pauses for a beat before grinning. "You know, we would get along pretty well if we were on the same side. I like you. No, really," he insists when I roll my eyes and scoff. "You're scrappy. I like that."

"Let me assure you, I couldn't possibly care less what you think about me. Let's cut the jokes," I suggest, folding my arms while Chief Perkins glowers at him beside me. Chief Perkins, who lost one of his guys last night.

I turned his way, noticing his stony stare. "Are you sure you want to be here for this?" I murmur, turning my head away from Viper.

The question seems to snap the man back into the present moment. "Yes, of course."

"I really don't know why you're wasting your time, and mine." As if to make a point, Viper yawns, letting his mouth open wide. I can't help but think about an actual viper, the way it opens its jaws and reveals its fangs. He is nowhere near as intimidating. "I already told you there are conditions to my speaking."

"That's right. You wanted a deal," I murmur, nodding slowly. "In fact, you demanded one if I remember correctly."

"You have a good memory." My skin crawls when once again, he looks me up and down. " You have a good … lots of things. We could get to know each other better, outside these circumstances."

He's looking to get a rise out of me, but he won't. I see him for what he is, who he is, and I am not impressed.

I look to the chief. "When was the last time a nurse was in here to offer a dose of medication for post-op pain?" I ask.

The chief looks at the clock opposite the bed. "Oh, it's been—"

"Four hours and fifteen minutes," Viper snaps. "And if anybody would answer this call, I could get another dose." He jams his thumb against the button to summon the nurse.

The chief and I exchange a look. He raises an eyebrow. I give my head a tiny shake. *Let me handle this.* It's obvious there is only one way to get through to this man, and I am certainly not about to play his game. There won't be a deal. Not if I have anything to say about it. He doesn't deserve it. For all we know, he was the one who gunned down a veteran officer last night.

"Why don't you go and see what's taking the nurse so long?" I suggest to the chief, who quirks an eyebrow but seems all too glad to leave the room. I don't blame him. I don't like being anywhere near this cretin, myself.

Once we're alone, my humorless smile drops away. "Here's how we stand," I tell him. "The rest of your stay at this hospital can pass easily, or every last minute can be excruciating for you."

"You think you're the first person to ever threaten me?" he asks with a dry laugh. "Please. If you think this is going to make a difference, you're going to be disappointed."

The sweat that's begun beading on his upper lip tells another story. "The pain is becoming a problem, isn't it?" I ask, remembering the look in his eyes when he thought I was about to be gunned down from behind. The way he smiled. How cruelly he shot those two officers outside the warehouse, the first time our paths crossed. The disregard he has for human life.

"I can handle pain," he assures me.

"You sure about that? Because from what I understand, that is a very painful wound you sustained last night." I click my tongue, shake my head in mock sympathy when he grimaces after moving to prove he can manage. It's almost too easy to manipulate him, but then it always is when bullies are involved. That's all he is.

"So what are you saying?" he grunts, his teeth gritted. "You're gonna torture me into telling you what you want to hear?"

Gripping the foot of the bed, I grit my teeth the way he grits his. "I want to know what you did with Ryan McAllister. We have the baby, we need the father. Where is he?"

"You have to ask someone who knows."

"Fair enough. I'll have to ask somebody who knows when you'll receive your next dose, too." With a glance toward the glass wall, I lift a shoulder. "It's looking pretty busy out there. From what I understand, two of the cops your people shot last night are still here, being treated. It could be everyone's too busy taking care of them to keep track of your needs. Wouldn't that be a shame?"

His expression doesn't shift, but his thumb continues attacking the call button like that's going to make a difference. "You're bluffing," he decides.

"That's what you're going with? Fine by me. We'll see if you're right." I back away from the bed, shrugging, then slowly walk toward the door. "Enjoy your stay. We'll reconnect once you're released."

I've opened the door and am ready to step through when he makes a choking sound. "Wait. Just wait. You know, I can tell my lawyer about this. I can have your badge."

"For what?" I ask, my head tipping to the side when I turn back to face him. "What did I say?" Am I proud of myself? Not really. Am I desperate enough to do this if it means bringing Ryan home? It seems that way. Maybe I'm sick of watching people like the man in front of me get away with everything they do. Not this time. He wants to play games? I can play games all day, and I am not the one handcuffed to a bed.

He attempts to stare me down, but it's no use. "Well?" I ask. "What did I say? What information could you give a lawyer that would jeopardize my career?"

I don't think I've ever engaged in a staring contest where the stakes were so high. I hold his gaze, waiting, patient if only for show. He blinks first, the way I knew he would, glancing toward the clock before licking his dry lips. "You'll make sure they come in and take care of me?" he asks, sweat now dampening his temples.

"I will. But I need you to tell me what I need to know, Viper. Where is he?"

A brief, bitter smile steals my breath before he murmurs, "He's someplace there's lots of people who don't appreciate what you did last night. And if you think you can get him out without losing more of your own, good luck."

"Give me the location, or all of this is moot." My hand closes around the door handle, prepared to pull.

"The old power plant," he blurts out. "At least,

that was the last place I saw him. They could've moved him by now—who's to say?" He is so desperate to make it look like he's still running things. I'd feel sorry for him if he were worth feeling sorry for.

"I remember seeing references to that location in some of the files we discovered."

His nostrils flare while his upper lip lifts in a quick, icy sneer before he remembers what's hanging in the balance and decides against whatever he was about to say. "Yeah, well, have fun trying to get your hands on him. You know, if the guys down there didn't already lose their patience."

"Thank you for the heads up." I need to get a team assembled, and quickly. I'm sure the man is messing with me, trying to get into my head, but there is a very real possibility Ryan has been moved by now. My knees are shaking as I slide the door open.

"Hey!" Viper barks. "You're sending somebody in, right?"

It's entirely possible I should not derive as much satisfaction as I do from turning around and offering a puzzled expression. "To do what?" Of course, I'm not going to get in the way of him getting what he needs, but I don't mind letting him think I will.

---

33

---

Alexis

---

I can't say I'm surprised when I arrive at the
rendezvous point and receive a report from the
advance team I sent to get eyes on the location.
"There's at least ten guys patrolling," Agent DeMeo
tells me before I've emerged from my car. "All armed."

"At least we know Viper's not sending us on some
wild goose chase, even if Ryan isn't inside." I truly
hope that's not the case. I hope this isn't another game
for him. When I think back on the sweat that was
almost rolling down his face by the time I left, I have
to imagine he was desperate enough to play along.

We've arrived at a location that plays a significant
role in this operation.

Minutes spent surveilling confirms the reports I
received on arrival. Armed men patrol the perimeter
of a power plant which, according to intel I requested
on my way from the hospital, has not been in operation in at least a decade. "Constant red tape issues," I
was told over the phone by Agent Morgan. "Locals

have been demanding they knock the place down for years now, since it's not in use, but the township keeps dragging its feet, hoping to rezone and turn it into something else."

Looking at it now, I can't imagine what. The structure looms like something out of a Gothic thriller, ominously backlit by sunshine that barely manages to pierce persistent cloud cover. It's going to rain soon, the smell of it hanging in the air. I hope we can get this over with before it starts to pour. There is enough evidence of crumbled structures behind the rusted chain-link fence that I wonder how much of the place still provides protection from the elements.

"Forrest, come in." Agent Morgan's voice crackles on my radio, which I pull from the car to respond. "We have some additional intel here. It seems the location was raided a few years back, when the DEA received word there was processing taking place inside. Undocumented young women, for the most part, basically forced into slave labor for the sake of protection and shelter."

"Let me guess," I mutter, staring at the plant. "They weren't able to make any charges stick."

"It's almost like you've done this before," he replies. Though I chuckle, there's no humor in it. How long can these people get away with this before somebody stops them? And Mitch wonders why I tend to take things on my shoulders? Somebody has to.

With that information in mind and the possibility of there being innocent people inside—Ryan included

—it's on me to formulate a plan that won't leave anyone in harm's way.

Someone managed to get their hands on blueprints for the plant which we pore over after spreading them out on the hood of my car. "You can see here." Agent DeMeo taps his fingers against the plans while I shine my phone's flashlight on the page to get a better look. "There are two levels of underground tunnels and rooms. Then look at this." He spreads a series of printouts over the top of the blueprints. "Satellite captures. This is six months ago, one year, eighteen months. Notice anything?"

"Construction materials," I muse, looking from the images to the structure in the distance. "It doesn't look like anything was changed on the surface."

"Exactly. It's likely they outfitted the lower levels. They could be holding people hostage in there, forcing them to work for their lives. Anything is possible," he concludes, grim.

Everyone is looking to me for answers, and there is only one I can offer. The only one that makes sense. "How many of us are here?" I ask, looking around.

"A dozen, so far, with another four cars on their way."

Four cars full of officers who most likely are wearing the same tape over their badges in remembrance of their fallen comrade. "They're looking for a fight," I murmur, keeping my voice slow so only DeMeo can hear. "We have to be careful."

It's not another fifteen minutes before the rest of the cars arrive and I give the entire team the rundown on what we're about to do. "Chances are high there's a lot of people inside," I conclude. "Innocents forced into labor. On top of that, we have at least a dozen armed guards patrolling the area. There will be more inside. I want everyone to test their radios now, secure body armor, and be ready to move in five."

By the time we begin our approach, fat raindrops have begun to hit my windshield. They soon turn into a steady drizzle while the team pours into the compound through three separate entrance points.

"Do not shoot to kill unless necessary," I remind everyone before the first shots are fired within moments of us leaving our vehicles.

Everything happens very quickly after that, with adrenaline pumping through my system and seemingly speeding up time while also slowing it down. I see everything so clearly; the vibrant red splash of blood on the ground as one of the operation's guards falls, clutching a wound to his left shoulder. The terror-filled eyes of a kid who can't be more than sixteen years old dropping his weapon and raising his hands into the air. "Don't shoot!" he begs before being overtaken by officers who get him on the ground to cuff him.

We are inside before the interior guards have received word of our arrival—at least, that's my assumption thanks to how surprised the men seem. Two of them have been playing cards, while a third was sacked out on his back, a rifle on the floor beside the sagging couch he's resting on.

"Hands!" I bark while officers flood in behind me.

They take care of the men while I continue with Agent DeMeo over my shoulder. This is the administration building from the looks of it, meaning there are countless abandoned offices where people can hide.

After giving each room a cursory search and finding nothing more than broken furniture and dust, we take the back stairs down to the first of two lower levels. "Soundproof," DeMeo notes. "Thick walls. They probably don't know what's going on upstairs, unless someone gave them the heads up over a radio."

After taking a deep breath to steady myself, I turn the knob and pull the door open for DeMeo to burst through, looking up and down the long, narrow hall before waving me on behind him.

An armed man bursts around the corner—his speed tells me someone got word out that we've arrived. When he raises his gun and takes aim, DeMeo responds with a shot to the man's shoulder. He goes down with a loud cry which will no doubt alert others to the trouble going down.

The hall splits off in two directions from the place where the armed man fell. DeMeo and I exchange a look before he waves four officers along behind him and heads to the left.

I take the other three and head right, checking one room after another and finding most of them empty except for cots, bedding, evidence people have been living here. I notice buckets on the floor and try not to imagine what they represent. These people don't even have access to toilets?

There are voices further down the hall, music playing, orders barked. I look over my shoulder toward the officers behind me and wave them on, prepared for whatever comes next. I have to believe we're prepared.

A bullet whizzes close to my head moments after we burst into the room lit by overhead fluorescents and filled with one long table after another. Women work with protective masks covering the lower half of their faces, latex gloves on their hands while they package white powder.

Our sudden presence brings their work to a halt. There's a moment when everyone freezes–it's almost comical, the way we stare at each other for what feels like forever but can't be more than a second or two.

Until I take note of the armed men positioned near the walls. "Get down!" I bark before taking aim at the nearest guard and bringing him down before he can do the same to me. Women shriek, scrambling for cover while we exchange fire.

When the smoke clears, one of ours is wounded while a handful of theirs run from the room, firing at random behind them and sending bullets flying while the screaming continues. "Stay down," I urge the women as I run through the room. There are so many women.

DeMeo catches up to me along with a pair of officers while the others clean up the mess. "Nothing but rooms the other way," he reports, though the way he snarls tells me there's more to it before he adds, "Some babies in cribs, tended by a kid who can't be more than eight or nine."

More babies. They're on my mind as we continue searching, disarming a pair of guards who look like they were on the verge of trying to get out when we found them. "Where is Ryan McAllister?" I demand once they're zip tied and no longer a threat. "Is he still being held here?"

"If I tell you," a thin, trembling young man asks, "will you go easy on me? I didn't do anything. I only guarded stuff."

"Where is he?" I ask again, leaning down, putting myself in his face so he can't look away. There's no avoiding the truth of who he's involved with, no matter how innocent he claims to be.

"Downstairs," the other man grunts. He's wounded, something I didn't notice before—one leg of his jeans is turning purple thanks to the blood he's losing. "There's a few guys on him."

I look toward DeMeo, who leads the way to another stairwell which we quickly descend before stepping into the basement. Pipes run overhead, air ducts and the like, lit only by bare bulbs hanging at even intervals. Up ahead, a door sits open and voices pour out from inside.

"Go, go! Got to get out of here." The voices get louder the closer we come, and before we can reach the room, a pair of men emerge.

It isn't the men themselves who make my heart stop. It's the man between them, his arms hanging over their shoulders, his body sagging when he can't support himself.

A very bruised, beaten man whose clothes hang on him like sails, as if he's lost a lot of weight in a short amount of time. "Stop right there." With my gun trained on them, and DeMeo backing me up, I grunt, "We're taking him out of here. If you know what's good for you, you'll let him go without a fight."

Ryan lifts his head slowly, and it sounds like he's fighting for every breath he takes. "Please … " he breathes before his head drops.

"This isn't worth dying for," DeMeo tells the men currently exchanging worried looks. They obviously agree with him, letting Ryan drop to the floor before they raise their hands.

# 34

# Alexis

Broken ribs along his right side, as if he was thrown onto a hard surface with his hands tied behind his back. A sprained wrist and three broken fingers. Dehydration, malnourishment. In the grand scheme of things, though Ryan McAllister is in pretty bad shape after his rescue, things could've gone much worse.

"Thank you. Thank you so much." A weeping Jessica has barely stopped thanking me after a tearful reunion with her barely conscious husband. "How can I thank you enough? You gave me my family back. No matter what, no matter where this started, I have my husband and my baby again." She throws her arms around me in an impulsive hug that I accept gratefully.

"I'm just glad we were able to find him before they changed locations. And I'm glad he wasn't hurt any worse." Peering through the glass door, I see Ryan lying in bed, sleeping now that all the tests have been run and the scans performed. I can only imagine the level of exhaustion he's dealing with. How much rest can a person get when they're being held captive?

It's Ethan who tugs at my heartstrings, sitting next to the bed with his head resting close to his dad's legs. His eyes are closed, but he wears a smile.

Jessica turns to me and it seems for the first time she's seeing me clearly. "You must be half dead on your feet by now. You really should get some sleep, Agent Forrest. You've been working around the clock to bring my family back together."

She isn't wrong. "It's all part of the job." Still, I find it difficult to stifle a yawn. It's no secret I need sleep, even with the mountains of new evidence and witnesses we discovered hours ago.

Glancing into Ryan's room, I murmur, "If he wakes up tonight, let him know I'll be back in the morning. I hate to make it seem like I'm bombarding him, but I will want to ask questions while everything's fresh in his mind."

"Of course. I'm sure he'll tell you anything you want to know. He has to just be so happy this is over." I don't have the heart to tell her she might be getting ahead of herself—all the evidence we have points to Ryan as being part of the very group that could've killed him. She's so happy. I don't want to burst her bubble.

Besides, thinking about home and how hard I've worked lately has me longing for bed and my pillow and my boyfriend, who will be waiting for me. My heart is full of warmth by the time I leave the hospital and point the Corolla toward home. Everything else can wait until tomorrow.

———

"Ryan?" To give him space and make him feel comfortable, I wait outside the room after seeing Jessica and Ethan head down to the cafeteria. I've been waiting, hoping to get him by himself, but it would feel cruel to ask Ethan to leave us alone when the kid is so obviously over the moon delighted that his father has returned.

Ryan looks away from the TV, where he's been trying to find something to watch. "Oh. Hello. I've been hoping I could thank you for getting me out of there." He sets the remote down, touching his head to the pillow behind it. "By all means, come on in."

A good start. I do as he asks, eyeing the flowers decorating the windowsill. "You have a lot of people very happy to know you're safe now," I observe with a smile. "How are you feeling?"

"Grateful. Exhausted," he admits, and we share a knowing chuckle. "To be honest with you, everything is so foggy. I keep trying to make sense of things, but they always kept me in the dark—literally. I never knew what day it was, what time it was. The disorientation alone was torture."

"I can only imagine. And you must've been worried," I add, watching him closely to gauge his reaction.

He winces, then nods. "I kept telling myself the

baby would be all right. They had no reason to hurt her."

"I'm so glad you were right." I pause, drawing a breath, then ask what I came here to ask. "You realize we understand you have shared history with this group who held you and your daughter."

His eyes narrow ever so slightly, but he nods. "Yes. Jess told me you found the information in my office."

"I want to say here and now that in the long run, we are more interested in learning about these people, their activities, their crimes. Any information you can provide will help us—and you," I make it a point to add. Pulling my phone from my pocket, I ask, "Is it all right if I record this? It'll be important for me to go back and keep track of names and locations."

He eyes the phone, then clears his throat. "I really don't know very much. I wasn't part of things for very long, either."

So he's still going with that explanation, though I've already made it clear we have all of his materials. "I understand, but we've been working on this case ever since you went missing. We've uncovered a lot of information, we have a lot of names and places. You never know what might help us tie them together, so please, don't try to censor yourself." I start a recording, then place my phone on the wheeled table positioned across his legs.

He glances at it before clearing his throat again. "I don't really know what to say. I helped smuggle materials in, disguising them as part of shipments I needed for new projects. The contractors used to build the projects employ a lot of people on the group's payroll, guys who don't really know anything about building, but handle the incoming shipments and that sort of thing. Guys on the inside. And I made sure what got sent over to them actually made it to them."

"You handled numbers and logistics."

"Right. That's exactly right. If something was late or a little light, I heard about it."

"From whom?"

He shrugs. "Higher ups."

"Such as? I'm looking for names," I explain quietly. "Please, be as specific as you can."

"Like I said, I didn't know that many people, I wasn't part of a lot of it. They keep it that way on purpose," he adds, licking his lips like they're suddenly dry. The words come out faster, too. "The fewer people you know, the fewer people you can incriminate later."

"What about Viper?" I ask, switching tracks. The light that suddenly flickers on behind his eyes tells me I've hit a nerve. "Did you ever deal with him?"

"Most of the time, yes." He almost smiles in what looks like relief. "He always knew all the specifics. He was in charge of a lot of things. A pretty scary guy," he adds.

"I don't know him anywhere near as well as you do, and I can certainly agree."

"Yeah, I've known him a long time," he murmurs with a grimace. "He's always been sort of scary. I'm sure it seems much worse to a stranger."

"Law enforcement, on top of that," I point out.

"Can you give me information on any locations you used to visit? We've already raided a few places, including the power plant in which you were found. Can you provide any more information?"

"There's the warehouse down by the Postal Service shipping hub. That was where I did most of my work, adding product to various shipments or retrieving it as needed. There's the old warehouses down on the wharf—sometimes, product would come through on boats, like private yachts to avoid notice from the authorities."

Still vague, but a possibility we hadn't looked into very deeply yet. I'll have to make a note of that. "What about anything you might have heard while you were captive?" He frowns and sighs, but I double down on my request. "You must've heard something. Names, plans?"

"Really, no. They didn't do much talking about things like that in front of me." He looks and sounds haunted by the memories.

My teeth grind thanks to the frustration I'm battling, but I manage to suppress the feeling. "Did they ever tell you why they took you? What were the circumstances of your kidnapping? Can you take me on a play-by-play of the night you went missing?"

When his face goes blank, the hair on the back of my neck lifts. "I ... I was called away."

"By whom?" I ask, almost holding my breath. There's something wrong here. His demeanor has changed too dramatically. He won't look at me. If his jaw gets much tighter, he'll break his teeth.

"You know what I kept asking myself all those days?" I almost can't hear him, he's whispering so softly. "Why?"

After a few silent beats, I prompt, "Why you were kidnapped?"

His head shakes ever so slightly. "Why they kept me alive."

"Sweetheart?" Jessica stops short in the doorway, holding a paper cup with a straw sticking out through a hole in the lid. "I brought you a milkshake. Chocolate." It's me she's looking at, though, wariness holding her in place.

"Oh, thanks. You remembered, I said I was craving one." Ryan sits up a little straighter, wincing and favoring the broken ribs on his right side. "I was just telling Agent Forrest everything I can remember, but there isn't much. I think I'm wasting her time."

"Oh, I wouldn't put it that way," I tell him before smiling at Jessica. "Like I told Ryan, you never know what will end up being the one fact that breaks the case open. Well, I don't think I used those words, exactly," I add, chuckling.

"And we are still so grateful for everything you've done." She takes the milkshake to Ryan, placing it on the table, eyeing my phone before looking at me.

"Trying to keep track of things." I almost forgot it was still recording. Retrieving it, I end the recording before sliding the phone into my pocket once again. "I'll leave you alone now. You have so much to catch up on."

For the sake of maintaining composure, I bite my

tongue before adding, "I'll be back." Because I certainly will.

This time, I'll have to visit while Jessica isn't in the building to interrupt us.

# 35

# Alexis

"Something's not adding up." With a sigh, I push back from the desk, folding my hands over the top of my head. My muscles are stiff after sitting in the same position for hours, combing through Ryan's often conflicting stories, trying to find the truth at the center of it all.

Chief Perkins stands in the doorway, leaning against the frame while stirring a cup of coffee. "What are you thinking?" he asks, chewing the plastic stirrer rather than drinking from the cup. Some people have habits like that which they engage in when they're thinking.

"That's just it. I don't know what to think anymore," I admit. "Between you and me, it's cases like this that leave me wondering what I'm doing in this career. It doesn't matter whether I have great instincts or not. I can't figure out how to tie everything together, so what difference does it make whether or not I know somebody is lying?"

"Time out." Tossing the stirrer into the wastebasket, he folds his arms, shooting me a curious look. "You think Ryan is lying?"

"He is certainly not being completely honest. Look at these notes I typed up." I motion for him to join me behind the desk, where I've pulled up transcripts of his statements so far. "He contradicts himself again. He wasn't involved with the ring for very long, but not three minutes later he talks about knowing Viper for a long time."

"Let's not forget what he's been through," Perkins points out. When I narrow my eyes, skeptical, he shrugs. "It's worth considering. That's all I'm saying."

"And all I'm saying is, when I look back through this, and when I listen to the recordings I made, it's clear to me that he was pulling information out of thin air sometimes. Other times, he was reciting facts, like I was quizzing him and he had the answers prepared."

Throwing my hands into the air, I ask, "What do you think? I know you went in to see him yesterday, too. Did anything about him strike you as odd?"

He releases a deep breath and eventually nods. "Sure. I noticed he seemed jumpy, unsure of himself. I chalked it up to him knowing he's going to be in a world of trouble after what he's done. Missing person or no missing person, there is a mountain of evidence pointing toward a long-time association with these people. Of course, he'll be nervous. He'll contradict himself. He struck me very much as someone hoping to say the right thing. The right combination of words, delivered the right way."

"I'm not satisfied with that," I decide. "I'm just not. He was already told before he started to make a statement that the more he cooperates, the easier it will be for him. We have no evidence of him being involved in violence. He's a pencil pusher for these guys. All he has to do is tell us what we need to know and he'll get a slap on the wrist. But that still wasn't enough to make him forthcoming."

Finally, light flicks on behind his eyes before he stands up straighter. "He's not afraid of incriminating himself. He's afraid of somebody."

"Exactly what I was thinking." I can't pretend it isn't hugely gratifying that we are finally on the same page. "Agent Childs offered him protection on the Bureau's behalf, promised he never has to go anywhere near these people again, except when he sees them in court. He promised protection for the family. And still, it was like pulling teeth to get Ryan to speak—and when he did, he'd go back and contradict himself practically in the next breath."

Finally, there's no way I can avoid sharing what I've kept to myself since yesterday morning. I don't want to jump to conclusions, but the more I go through my memory—aided by the recording I made —the clearer it is he was afraid. Not of Viper, though Viper could play a part in it. "I think Jessica has more to do with this than we know."

"The wife?" It's obvious from his reaction that he does not agree, almost laughing.

"Look at this." I pull out my phone to show him several photos I took while going back through the coded ledger. "This is what I found at the motel. Look at all of these initials. Look at the pair that keeps showing up over and over. JM."

"All right, Jessica McAllister," he allows. "But there are plenty of names with those initials."

"I'm telling you. She knows something about all of this. Let's go back to her first statement," I insist when the chief clicks his tongue like he disagrees. "She talked about being asleep while he took the baby out. She talked about the secret phone calls Ryan has been getting. Was that a terrified wife putting two and two together, or was it a woman deliberately misdirecting us?"

At least he takes his time before shooting me down. "If his demeanor changed when his wife entered the hospital room yesterday, don't you think it could be just as likely he doesn't want her to hear about these things? Specifics?"

All right. I see his point. It takes a little of the fire out of me, but not much. "I'm going back to talk to him today, while Jessica is teaching. I called over to her school earlier," I admit. "Confirming she'll be there into the afternoon."

"You want to get him alone."

"Exactly." Gathering my things, I ask, "Care to join?"

"Are you kidding?" He rubs the back of his neck, wincing. "With all the work you dropped on my desk by going into that power plant? I barely know which end is up at the moment."

All through my drive to the hospital, I remind

myself of everything pointing me toward Jessica playing a bigger part in this than she has let on so far. What she described to me as Ryan's strange, secretive dealings could just as easily have been her own late-night phone calls.

And the disappearance of her baby could have been Viper's way of keeping her in line. A reminder of what's at stake if she crosses him.

There are countless possibilities running through my head by the time I reach the private room Ryan was transferred to once his doctor stepped him down from the ICU. It's still comfortable, but he doesn't require such close observation now. I hope that means he's feeling clear headed as I reach the room where he is reading a book.

"Anything good?" I ask, offering a brief grin as I enter.

"To be honest, I can't concentrate for long. I've read the same page three times." He closes the paperback, setting it aside. "What can I do for you?"

Before I say a word, I start a new recording on my phone. Setting it in front of him, I ask, "What were you doing the night you disappeared? You never did answer when I asked yesterday."

"Didn't I? It's all so foggy."

He has to know that excuse isn't going to work much longer. It barely works now. "What were you doing, Ryan? Why were you out with the baby so late at night, without telling your wife you were leaving?"

He's in pain, but it's nothing physical twisting his features into a grimace. "I got a call. I had to go out."

"A call from whom? Where were you going? What did Isabel have to do with it?" I can't stop myself. There's no stopping the flood of questions pouring from my mouth while he shrinks away. "Did someone request you bring her along? If so, why? Did you leave her at the motel? Or did someone take her there after you were taken?"

"I don't know." He closes his eyes slowly, tipping his head back. His throat works, his jaw clenches. "I don't know. Okay? I don't know what else to say."

"Why don't you know? What do you feel you can't tell me? We're alone here, Ryan. No one can hear you. You've already been offered protection. Tell me what I need to know, please." I didn't plan on adding a personal plea, but I'm desperate at this point. It's obvious there is so much more to this than what first met the eye.

"I was going to take both of them. I don't want you thinking I would only take Isabel and not Ethan. Ethan didn't want to go," he explains.

"Where were you going to take the kids?"

" To my parents house in Connecticut. I didn't want to separate Izzy from Jess, but it was the only way. I couldn't have them around her," he insists with quiet intensity. "And every day they spent in that house, they were in danger. They could still be in danger now. She swears they aren't."

"Why did you feel you had to leave?" I whisper.

"Because of what she's been doing. I didn't know until a few months ago, six at the most. It really is a blur. It was like the whole world ended. I didn't know until then that Jess was into this whole … I hate to say it. It sounds so ugly. Drug ring."

His eyes snap open and he hits me with a panicked stare. "How did I not know? She's my wife. I sleep next to her every night. Everybody who knows her thinks she's an angel—the most devoted teacher these kids ever had. And I find out she's been keeping books for these guys. And other things."

His tone darkens before he lowers his brow. "Recruiting. I can't believe I'm telling you this. Betraying her. But she betrayed our family. And I have to keep the kids safe."

I'm reeling, making it difficult to remain calm and ask the right questions. "What happened that night?" I prompt.

"She was holding the kids over my head." It looks and sounds like every word is torture. "Forcing me to work alongside these scumbags. Getting me into it so I couldn't break free without incriminating myself. Telling me this was all for them, to set them up for life. They'd never have to worry about a thing. She was pregnant at the time, and I didn't want to jeopardize either of them, so I went along with it … until I found out I was supposed to personally make a delivery the next day."

His throat works and a sickened look comes over his face. "Girls. She wanted me to deliver young girls to this filthy motel so they could work for the ring. That was the last straw. I knew I had to go, to at least get the kids far away from all of it."

He shakes his head. "Ethan wouldn't leave, the

stubborn kid. I was panicking. I left with the baby but was only halfway to town when Viper spotted me. I don't know how—she won't tell me, but I think Jess might have woken up and realized I was gone, then called him. Isabel was a little fussy as we were leaving. It could've woken her up. He almost ran me off the road, then forced me at gunpoint to let him into the truck. He told me where to drive. We stopped, somebody dragged me out of the truck and knocked me unconscious. The next thing I knew, I was waking up with my hands bound and a blindfold over my eyes."

His voice breaks, but he pushes through. "I was so scared for the baby. I told myself Izzy would be safe, that Jess would take her home again, but ... I just didn't know for sure. I don't know anything about her," he concludes, his voice heavy with sorrow.

Apparently, not many people know the real woman behind the smile and the perfect home.

But I'm about to make it my life's mission to know her inside and out. I'll have to if there's any hope of getting to the bottom of this.

# 36

# Alexis

"She's going to be spooked, being brought in like this." Chief Perkins blows out a sigh now that one of his deputies brought Keaton in for further questioning.

"Let her be spooked," I decide. "If she had been honest in the first place, we wouldn't have gone to all the trouble of bringing her back in."

Looking through the file I've put together, I locate Ryan's statements and reflect on how they pertain to her. "Ryan said girls were held at the motel as sort of a stop-off point before being transferred elsewhere. Some were trafficked, others were sent to that power plant to process packaging of narcotics. Some of these girls have babies who need minding—and sometimes," I conclude with a bitter grunt, "the children are held separate from the mothers to … what's the word he used? Motivate them." The idea makes me sick, but it also makes a sick sort of sense.

Still, I want a firsthand account, meaning there's nothing left to do but go in and question Keaton. She looks healthier than she did only days ago—her hair is clean and shining, she's wearing a tank top and sweater that look like they could be new. I'm sure her parents were happy to have her home. What a shame they might have to say goodbye again, depending on what I learn today and what it means.

"Hi, Keaton. How have you been?" Taking a seat across from her, I notice the way she scowls, even if the expression is short-lived.

She tucks her hair behind her ears, shrugging. "I'm kind of freaked out right now. I thought once I went home, that was it."

"I am sorry you were given the wrong information, but new facts have come to light. I need to discuss them with you."

"Yeah, well, I was supposed to have a job interview later on. I really don't want to miss it."

"I'll do what I can." Did the girl manipulate me all along, the way Jessica has? I can't let those suspicions color our interactions now, but it's a challenge to stay cordial and not give away anything too soon. "I don't know if you heard yet, but we located Ryan McAllister a couple of days ago."

"Yeah, I heard it on the news." Her body language speaks volumes – arms folding while she tucks her chin close to her chest.

"He has a lot to say, but then I guess you could assume that, too. We know a lot more about the hierarchy of the organization, who does what, that sort of thing. And one position we keep coming back to is somebody referred to as the minder. The one who minds the girls at the motel and watches any children who might be involved."

"Yeah, so?" Defiance leaks into her voice, into the way she looks at me. "Are you saying that's me? Is that why you brought me all the way back here?"

"I'm saying I need to know who that is. If it was you, we can work with you, help you with whatever comes next."

Her chin trembles. "What does that mean?"

"Keaton, it means you aided and abetted human trafficking, for starters."

"I didn't! I was only watching them—" It's almost comical the way her face falls once her brain catches up to her mouth and snaps it closed.

"Yes, that is exactly what you were doing," I murmur once she's had a moment to recover. "Who told you to take care of Isabel, after she was taken from Ryan? What were the conditions?"

Her face contorts in an expression of pure agony. She was so close to getting out of this unscathed, at least in her own mind. "Listen. I didn't want to, but I figured it was better for the kid. I was gentle with her. Some of the other girls don't have any patience, but I do. I figured so long as somebody was taking care of her, it was all right. I was doing a good thing."

"At whose command?" I ask. She scowls, averts her gaze, setting off a storm of frustration inside my skull. "Keaton, you have already wasted enough of my time. I was willing to give you the benefit of the doubt, but that time has passed."

"I don't know what you want from me!" she snaps.

"I want you to tell me the truth. Why is that so difficult for everyone to comprehend?" *Easy, now.* I have to take a breath, recenter myself, before this goes completely off the rails.

In a quieter tone, I continue. "I know you're afraid. I know these are bad people. But if you think you're going to get out of this without a scratch on you, I'm here to tell you you're wrong. Jessica McAllister was willing to pretend her own daughter was kidnapped in order to maintain the lie she's built up. What do you think she would do to you? I want you to really think about that," I insist when Keaton looks away. "Everyone always thinks they are exempt, somehow. Yes, I know I work for terrible people, but they would never do terrible things to me. Yet here we are, aren't we?"

"She was going to get me out. Okay? She told me this was my way out, if I did what she needed me to do."

"What was that?"

"I was supposed to watch the baby, the way I always watched the kids, going in and out. But even before then … " She chews her lip hard, shaking her head, almost whimpering before she continues. "She wanted me to keep an eye on him. Ryan. Like, watch him whenever he came to the motel to pick up or drop off, whatever. She said she thought he was about to punk out on her. And if I did what she needed me to do, she would give me enough money to get out of town and start fresh."

"Did you honestly think she would?"

"Did I have another choice? I had to believe her. It's not like I could say no," she adds, scoffing. "You don't get to say no to these people."

Yes, that seems to be a recurring theme. I have to sit back and catch my breath while she does the same. "You don't get it," she whispers, shaking her head. "There are a lot of people involved in this. Not just us —you know, me and the people you arrested at the motel. Regular people. Moms and dads. The people you see on the street every day. They want pills, they want powder. Jessica's not the only one who works for these guys—but I think she's maybe the one who makes them the most money. She's close with Viper, like they're friends or something."

This is news to me. Ryan never said anything about them having a personal relationship. "You're sure about that?"

"I've seen them talking together a lot, the way people do when they know each other. Not strangers, you know? She makes them a lot of money with pills, selling them to parents. And she's real smart, so she handles money and stuff like that. I think she brought Ryan in to work with her. She said it was just too much for her to handle on her own, but I had a feeling there was more going on. But it wasn't my business, you know?"

I can't sit here a minute longer. Not while there are so many questions now percolating like mad in the back of my head. "Sit tight," I tell her, standing, going to the door.

"I have my interview!"

275

"It's going to have to wait." Am I supposed to feel sorry for her now? She lied to me. Fear was a motivator, yes, but she's made things much more challenging for herself, and I can't pretend I'm not disappointed.

At the moment, however, there are bigger issues at hand. Chief Perkins and Agent Morgan are waiting for me in the chief's office, having observed the interrogation feed on the chief's computer.

"I don't understand. Why?" I close the door and lean against it, eyes shut, rubbing my temples. "Why would Jessica leave the baby at the motel instead of taking her home? Why involve her in any of this? If she knew Isabel was there the whole time—"

"You missed something. No offense, but you didn't ask the right question." Chief Perkins wastes no time moving me away from the door so he can leave the room and join Keaton across the hall, where she is sniffling pathetically while waiting for what comes next. We watch the feed, listening, as he asks, "Keaton, who told you to watch Isabel McAllister? Who gave you that job?"

"Viper. Viper brought her in in the middle of the night. He said if Jessica came, to call him right away. She wasn't allowed in the room, she wasn't allowed to see the baby."

How could I have missed that? "There are so many pieces to this case," Agent Morgan murmurs, almost like he's reading my thoughts. "We can't cover all the bases at once."

Now it makes sense in a twisted sort of way. "Maybe that was the last straw for Viper," I muse once the chief rejoins us. "He went out and stopped Ryan before he could get away. What if he decided to hold the baby as a way of making sure Jessica got things under control?"

"No more late-night calls to tell him something went wrong," Morgan muses, and I nod.

"He was warning her to get her house in order," Chief Perkins agrees. "I have to wonder why she got the authorities involved at all."

"It could've been their way of covering it all up," I suggest. "They probably didn't expect us to find him, or the baby. Not until they were ready for us to find them. But of course, if Ryan didn't show up to work, there would be questions. This was their way of controlling the narrative."

The more I think about it, the more sense it makes. There are still a lot of fundamental questions —at the forefront, how did Jessica get involved in any of this in the first place?

There's only one way to find out.

# 37

# Alexis

"We need this to be airtight. She cannot have any room to wiggle out of these accusations, which means shoring up our case. The narrative we've constructed."

Looking around the room, I find agents DeMeo, Morgan, and the others sent down from Portland by Special Agent Childs, who has joined us via Zoom to be part of our session. The past thirty-six hours have been a whirlwind of painstakingly digging through the fully decrypted files, pinpointing each instance where Jessica's initials were used.

"The communications from one of the flash drives point to her." DeMeo pinches the bridge of his nose between his thumb and forefinger—he's worked around the clock, determined to unlock the rest of the files so we can finally pin Jessica down. None of us could have seen this case ending this way, and I know there's a hint of regret in all of our minds. After all, this is a mother with children who depend on her. Though she has done terrible things, there is no joy in the idea of taking her from the kids.

I can't help but think of Ethan as I pull up a series of messages on a monitor mounted at the front of the conference room across the hall from Chief Perkins' office. "Checking in on the visitor," I murmur, reading aloud. "And the little visitor. Keep me posted if she needs anything."

"It has to be Isabel she's referring to," Agent Morgan says, looking around the room as the rest of us nod our agreement.

"According to Keaton, she was required to upload all of these chat logs, and save them on a regular basis," I remind everyone, scrolling through the seemingly endless log. "Granted, she was usually charged with keeping track of her communications with Ryan —at least, that was the original instruction Jessica gave."

"Jessica didn't figure the kid would be just as painstaking with the rest of her communications— including the ones between the two of them," Childs concludes. "Her instructions have come back to haunt her."

"Viper's real name is Vincent Malone." Opening his file, I skim the contents—not for the first time. Not even close. He grew up in Portland, the same as Jessica McAllister. Finding his legal name opened up the entire case. He and Jessica attended the same high school, growing up two blocks apart. "She went to college, he went to jail, but somewhere along the way they must have reconnected, because here we are."

"Which would explain Ryan knowing Viper for a long time. There's a chance they reconnected before Viper ever pulled Jessica into his business." Childs shakes his head slowly, going through the information I sent his way to catch him up before this meeting. "I wonder how long it took him to see how lucrative it would be, bringing Jessica in. She's the perfect front, beloved teacher, perfect wife, perfect mother. Exactly the sort of person no one thinks twice about."

I certainly didn't, did I? Granted, I could only go off of the information given to me at the time, but it never occurred to me for an instant Jessica might be steering me in one direction versus another, creating the narrative. Pinning everything on Ryan, playing the part of the distraught mother whose only concern was for her husband and child. If it hadn't been for Ryan's attempt at breaking free, I wonder how much longer this would have gone on. How much uglier it would have gotten.

"Here, we see the coded ledger entries featuring her initials." I pull up image after image. "Here, messages sent through Snapchat, detailing meetings and shipments. The account they come from is the same account whose owner communicated with Keaton about whether the so-called visitors needed anything."

"This, combined with Ryan's and Keaton's statements, are as strong a case as we're going to make against her with the evidence we've pieced together," Agent Childs concludes. There is no satisfaction in his voice. It's fatigue for the most part, plus something else

I identify with all too well. Disappointment. As satisfying as it is to build this case, drilling down until we get to the truth, there's sadness to it, as well. The chance of a family being pulled apart.

Then again, how many families has this organization pulled apart? But Ethan and Isabel aren't responsible for that. They are the ones who will lose out in the end.

Which is why, though I can't wait to bring Jessica in so I can present her with these statements and files, there's hesitation involved. Especially when I think back on Ethan sleeping with his head on Ryan's bed, smiling. Contented. All was right in his world.

"If anything," I conclude when it's just me and Childs after the others left the room, "I might be able to use the kids as leverage. If she wants to raise them herself, she has to come clean in a helpful, productive manner."

"Absolutely. At the end of the day," he concludes with a sigh, "she is a mother, and it does seem she cares about her children. Which is how you might be able to get her to work with us," he adds, arching his eyebrows.

"Meaning?"

"Meaning, we still don't know for sure why Isabel was taken to the motel rather than brought home. We can guess all we want, and we're probably on the right track."

"A way of keeping Jessica in line," I conclude.

He nods in response. "Exactly. She didn't have a choice, she did what she had to do for her children, that sort of thing. Remember. We are sympathetic, if only for the sake of gaining her trust."

That's the thing. It's not easy to be sympathetic when I remember how scared Keaton was when we first met. How intimidated she and all those other young women must have been. Then, there's the women working at the power plant, the children being minded in another room. For years, this ring has been profiting from the misery of others.

When I look at it that way, remembering Jessica had a choice not to become involved in this, my resolve hardens the way I need it to.

"I think we're ready to bring her in," I conclude, and it's gratifying when he nods his agreement.

"You have my approval, Agent Forrest. Have Chief Perkins send deputies to bring her in."

His eyes widen when I shake my head. "No, I think this would work better at home. So she's reminded of everything she's going to lose out on if she doesn't cooperate."

"Fair enough. I didn't think of it that way. Don't take any chances, though," he warns. "Let's not give her too much credit. Make sure there's backup waiting outside, and that she knows about them."

I agree before signing off, almost trembling in anticipation. Is he right? Would she do something desperate if it meant saving herself?

I guess there's only one way to find out.

# 38

# Alexis

"Agent Forrest." There is strain in Jessica's greeting, and it matches well with the strain on her face when she looks over my shoulder to find a marked car parked in the driveway, a deputy behind the wheel. "I was about to get dinner started. Isabel just went up for a nap."

"I understand." It's clear she expects me to say something more, maybe to assure her this won't take long, but I can't give her what she wants. "I have some questions for you. It really can't wait."

"Questions?" There's a kitchen towel hanging over her shoulder, which she now takes in hand and uses to wipe a smudge from the door frame. "I don't understand. Ryan and Isabel are safe. The doctor says he'll be home any day now. Maybe even tomorrow. What else could you possibly want from us?"

"Mrs. McAllister, respectfully, I was in your presence when I found the ledger and appointment book in your basement. The missing persons aspect of this case might be resolved, but the bigger case is ongoing."

"Well, you're going to have to solve it without us, because my family has already been through enough." She looks behind her back with a frown. "Ethan is finishing up his homework, and I have tests to grade while the chicken roasts."

I didn't want to have to do it this way, but she's left me no choice. "We know about your history with Vincent. That you reconnected after he was released from prison. You both grew up in a tough situation and it bonded you, and he used that shared past as a way of drawing you into his present business. Tell me I'm wrong," I conclude.

Her eyelids flutter and her face goes pale and for one moment, I'm afraid she's going to faint. "You don't know any of that for sure," she whispers, and her expression goes stony before my very eyes.

"But I do. We don't have to do this here, on the front porch. I can come in ... or you can come down to the station and we'll discuss it there."

When she hesitates, I have no choice but to pull out the big guns. "Nobody wants to see you taken from your children. I don't want it. I know you don't. The only way you can ensure that now is by cooperating fully. Telling me what I need to know, making it possible for us to put an end to this. Now I ask you," I add, "do you think you would have the chance to escape these people on your own? I'm giving you that opportunity now, and the opportunity to keep your children rather than being forced to hand them over to relatives—if there are any," I add. A cheap shot? Maybe. But it's also the truth. Either she does as we ask, or we take her in and process her, then either release her on bail or hold her until trial.

When she looks over my shoulder again, I murmur, "You can either let me in and we'll do this quietly, or I can escort you out to the car now. I'm sure you think it looks bad, a police car in your driveway. How much worse will it look if I have to take you with me?"

"Fine. Come in—but please," she whispers. "Do not let Ethan know. All right? That's the one thing I ask."

"You don't have to worry about that."

She must believe me, since she opens the storm door to let me inside. "Hey, buddy?" she calls out, leading the way through her miraculously clean first floor. "How about you finish that up after dinner?"

Ethan looks up at us from his spot on a stool at the kitchen island. "Oh, hi," he says, smiling at me. "Did you hear anything about my dad? When is he coming home?"

"Agent Forrest isn't a doctor or nurse, remember? We already talked about this," Jessica explains. The tenderness in her voice reminds me there are so many different sides to people. No one is entirely one thing or another. As I watch, she runs a hand over her son's head—this isn't an out-of-character interaction, either.

He doesn't flinch away, doesn't shoot her a puzzled look. She isn't doing this for my benefit. She's doing it for his, and maybe her own.

"We won't be long," I promise Ethan, leaving out the part where it's really up to his mother how long this takes. He gathers his things and leaves the room, and soon his footsteps ring out on the stairs.

She turns to me, her back against the counter, folding her arms. "I don't know why you bothered coming here. You already seem to think you know everything."

"Maybe I'm giving you the chance to tell your side of the story."

Scoffing, she turns her head to look out the window. "Don't give me that. Don't pretend you're my friend."

"Fine. We can do this your way." I pull out my phone, begin a new recording, set it on the counter. Frankly, I'd rather get this over with than keep on with pleasantries. "Do you or do you not have a past personal relationship with Vincent Malone, otherwise known as Viper?"

Her brow wrinkles. "You already know."

"I want to hear it from you, Jessica."

"Yes," she spits. "We grew up together, went to high school together, but our lives went in different directions. Until he found me here after he was released from prison. He needed a way to expand his business and he knew a suburban mother with ties to the community would be perfect."

"What made you say yes?"

"He made it sound easy. Like I would barely have to do anything." Her jaw twitches before she runs a hand under her eyes. "You never know how deep they've sucked you in until it's too late. That's how they survive, you know? It's either cooperate, or you're finished. You and your family and everyone you care about."

I'm not ready to fall for that story just yet. She's already manipulated me. "What did he offer?"

"Money, of course. What, you don't know how difficult it is to live on a teacher's salary? And Ryan's business … it's good, but there are ebbs and flows. We were swinging between feast and famine for so long. This meant starting education funds for the kids and actually contributing to them instead of having to take all the money out to pay the bills when business was slow. It meant the end of all of our problems—and yes, I can look back now and see how stupid it is, thinking that way, but that's the beauty of hindsight, isn't it?"

"How did Ryan find out? How long had it been before he did?"

Now, she's in pain. Going stiff, standing up straighter, lifting her chin like she's defiant of her very memories. "Vincent approached me around two years ago. We wanted to have another baby, but there was no guarantee we'd be able to handle the bills. Vincent promised all this money. Security. And it was so easy on paper."

She draws a shuddering breath, her arms tightening around her middle. "Of course, things escalated. It went from identifying buyers to doing the selling myself. Then, he wanted me to oversee a handful of other women like me, distributing for him. He called it a promotion," she adds with a bitter chuckle.

The chuckle dies, silence following. "I was in too deep by then. I got pregnant, I told him I wanted to step back and not be as involved. You know what he did? He looked me in the eye—remember, we've known each other all these years—and said wouldn't it be a shame if something happened to you while you're carrying that kid?"

Of this, I have no doubt. The man smiled when he thought he was about to watch me die. "He was threatening the baby."

"Right." She wipes away another tear. "There was my answer. There was no stepping back. I knew I wouldn't be able to keep a secret from Ryan forever, not with Vincent constantly giving me more responsibilities, pulling me in deeper. It was one thing when I was only distributing to moms, parents at the school. But it was more money, too, and I tried to tell myself it was worth it so long as the kids can have a good future. Really, sometimes that was all I had, but Ryan did find out," she mutters with a sigh, staring at the floor.

I don't dare say a word while she's in this flow state, letting the story take shape without any guidance. It seems now she's started, there's no stopping.

"Can you believe he actually tried to confront Vincent about it? He told him to let me go. I still don't know if that was brave or stupid, to be honest with you. And all Ryan ended up doing was getting himself caught up along with me. I had no choice but to make him fall in line, because I knew what Vincent would do if he didn't. To me, the kids, all of us. They are so good at taking away. That's how they survive."

After a few long, silent moments, I ask, "What happened that night? Why did you call the police? Why alert the authorities at all?"

Her cheeks go red, then her nose, before the tears start to flow steadily. "Ethan. He woke up. He heard me on the phone. I called Vincent right away—I heard Ryan leaving with Izzy, I looked out the window and I could see the truck pulling away. I panicked. I knew he was running. He didn't want to follow orders anymore. So I called Vincent for help, because I was afraid somebody even worse than he is would find them and get rid of them."

She wipes away her tears with a shaking hand. "Only Ethan heard me. He knew his dad and his sister were missing, but he didn't know why. I had to do something, explain it somehow."

"But you didn't call it in until hours afterward, right?"

"Obviously, I had to wait. I wasn't going to call the police without putting some kind of plan together. Vincent told me it was the only way. That I had to tell the authorities exactly what he demanded, or ... "

I have a feeling what's coming next, but I will not put the words in her mouth. Let her offer them up.

"Or I would never see Izzy again," she concludes. "That's why he was holding her. To keep me quiet. There was always the chance he would sell her off and I would never see her again. Do you think I could let that happen?"

"Of course, anybody would fight to keep their baby safe." My understanding seems to unlock something in her. She covers her face with her hands as sobs wrack her. I watch, strangely devoid of emotion. There's no anger, but there's no sympathy, either. I don't think I have room anymore.

Once she quiets down, I murmur, "We need names. All the names you know. All of the information you might be holding back. You're low level—we both know that," I point out.

Her hands drop so she can train her wide, bloodshot eyes on me. "I'll tell you anything. Absolutely anything, I swear. So long as there's no chance of them coming for us. Any of us. I just want my family back."

I won't be the one to tell her. I'm not sure she'll ever get her family back, not the way it was before. Not when Ryan feels so betrayed, like he can't trust her. He'll never look at her the same way.

Still, there's more of a chance of her getting her family back while she's not in prison. "We're going to do everything we can, I promise. Your family will be protected. As for charges, I can't make any promises on behalf of the District Attorney's office, but we will recommend a plea deal. The more you give us, the sweeter it can be for you."

"I'll call my lawyer." With her chin quivering, whispers, "Please. My kids need their mom."

"I know they do—but it's up to you," I remind her before ending the recording so I can make the necessary phone calls.

# 39

## Alexis

"I still don't understand what the problem is with primer gray." Mitch rests the paint roller in the pan, where a deep shade of blue paint waits to be spread across the living room wall.

"Primer gray is what contractors use. You aren't supposed to actually keep the color on the wall. It's a starting point," I remind him. This is not the first time we've had this conversation ever since he suggested we do a little redecorating for my sake. So I can feel more at home rather than feeling like I'm living in his home. Sure, he keeps finding reasons to grumble, but I know that's only on the surface. He's doing this with the best intentions.

The blue is going to look perfect on the walls, where sunlight will turn it into sapphire. It will go well with the gray slipcover we purchased for the sofa, with the rich golden yellow for the armchairs and throw pillows in a matching shade. "I can't wait to see it when it's all done," I confess, almost squealing with excitement before dipping the roller into my paint tray.

"Careful. Don't load up the roller too much or it's going to turn out all lumpy and streaky."

Somehow, I manage to keep from rolling my eyes too hard. "I know what I'm doing, you know. If I have any questions about baking or the correct temperature for roasting coffee beans, I will be sure to ask you."

"You're so charming when you get sassy like that." He joins me, draping an arm around my waist while I roll paint onto the wall. It's a very satisfying process, made more enjoyable by the fact that he cut-in the corners for me. I've never been any good at that, always leaving streaks along the ceiling no matter how hard I try not to.

"See? It wasn't too much." I turn to him wearing a defiant smirk and am rewarded by him touching a finger to the tip of my nose—when he pulls it away, I find the dark blue paint staining his skin.

"You jerk!" I take a swipe and come back with a streak of paint on the back of my hand. "That's how you want to play? Are you sure you want to? I've got a whole gallon of paint here, my friend."

"Go ahead. Everything's covered in plastic." He extends his arms to the sides, indicating the protective plastic sheets we laid over the furniture and floor. "No better time than now to get out any tensions."

It's a tempting thought, but … "We wanted to get this done by the end of the day, remember? So it'll be dry tomorrow and we can start hanging things on the walls. I know I'm taking time off, but I can't take off forever. And there were other things we wanted to do," I conclude, kissing his cheek.

"Fair enough. I'm not going to squander the time I have with you." He wanders back to his side of the room. "And I guess I don't need all that paint in the pipes, once we shower it off."

Now that so many of the drug ring's high-level players have been identified and arrested, there's never been a better time than the present to take the vacation I'm so desperately in need of. It's cases like this that leave me requiring a reset, or as close to one as I can manage. Cases that leave me with a little less faith in humanity than I had before. Special Agent Childs was completely in favor of it, which comes as no big surprise. He's been urging me to take time off for weeks now.

"You know what would look great on this wall?" Mitch asks after finishing a coat of paint on the wall the sofa sits against. "Remember that poster we found? All thirty-two pro football teams, right here." He holds his arms out like he's imagining the poster's size and where he'll place it on the wall.

"I know you're joking, so I'm not going to react."

"What? You're the one who got on my case about my ... what was it? Minimalist decorating?"

"Close enough," I confirm with a snort.

"So let's add something interesting. Something that will draw the eye." He can barely stifle his laughter while I roll my eyes and shake my head.

"I was thinking more along the lines of a gallery wall. Framed photos, memories. We can both add our own, you know? Sort of a symbol of our lives blending together." I look over my shoulder while reloading my roller and find him smiling softly. "What? Thinking about the next place you want to smear paint?"

"I wasn't, but I am now." Chuckling, he joins me, gently removing the roller from my hands and setting it aside before wrapping his arms around me. "I was thinking more along the lines of how lucky I am. Yes, that sounds like the perfect idea. A visual reminder of how we've joined our lives. I love it. We'll have to start looking through photos."

"I can hardly wait."

Our kiss is interrupted by my ringing phone, a sound that makes us both groan. "Everybody at work knows to step back and give me some space," I vow, holding up my right hand. "So if somebody's calling, it's probably Mom or Dad."

"I guess I can't ask you to ignore a call when you put it that way." Still, he kisses me again, until my heart sinks as I free myself from his embrace. Of all times for somebody to pick up the phone. Then again, they might've done us a favor—there is still plenty of painting to be done, and Mitch is much too distracting.

"Unknown number?" I groan. "That's the third time I've gotten a call from an unknown number today. You'd think they'd leave a voicemail if it's important enough." I set the phone down, shaking my head and grumbling at the interruption, going back to my paint roller so we can finish this up.

A soft buzz from the phone tells me they did, in

fact, leave a message this time. I should let it go. I know I should. There's nothing so important it can't wait.

Noticing my hesitation, Mitch sighs. "For heaven's sake." He dips his roller into my paint tray so he can finish the rest of my wall. "Find out who it was. Now you have me curious."

"I'm sure it's nothing important." I open the voicemail and hold the phone to my ear, waiting to hear something about my car's extended warranty. Something pointless like that.

Only that isn't what's waiting for me. "Agent Forrest, please, forgive me. I jumped through hoops to get my hands on your cell number, which is something I would never do unless there was an emergency. My name is Rosamund Malone, and I'm an editor at a publishing house with a client who's gone missing. Elizabeth Kovalenko. The local police have done nothing to find her, though I'm sure something is very wrong."

He hesitates, and I hold my breath in anticipation. "We're usually in constant contact. She is never uncommunicative. She writes thrillers—maybe you've heard of her. The current manuscript she's working on has tied her up for weeks, but she's always kept in touch. I received a strange message from her a week ago. She told me she'd uncovered a real-life conspiracy that happens to mirror what she's been writing in her latest book. Since then, it's been radio silence. She's vanished."

There goes the hair on the back of my neck,

standing straight up. My hand tightens around the phone as he concludes, "Agent Forrest, I read about your involvement in that missing persons case that was recently closed. I hear you're tenacious. I need someone with tenacity to take me seriously, because I know Elizabeth is in trouble. Right now, you might be the only person who can help."

---

Thank for you reading Forest of Regrets. Can't wait to find out what happens to Alexis next? **Get Forest of Deception Now!**

When FBI Agent Alexis Forrest receives an unexpected voicemail from a desperate book editor, she never imagines it will lead her into a deadly web of fiction turned reality.

**A star bestselling author has vanished without a trace after claiming she's uncovered a real-life conspiracy matching the plot of her latest thriller.**

Just as Forrest is settling into life in the quaint New England town of Broken Hill and moving in with Mitch—her high school sweetheart turned local bookstore owner—she finds herself drawn into a dangerous investigation that the local police have dismissed.

As the lines between imagination and truth begin

to blur, Forrest must determine if Elizabeth's manuscript holds the key to her disappearance—or if it will become her obituary. The peaceful charm of Broken Hill may be exactly what Forrest needs to start over, but first, she'll have to survive this case.

**1-click Forest of Deception now!**

---

## 🌑 NEW SERIES ANNOUNCEMENT 🌑

FBI Agent River Collins knows firsthand the terror of being taken. Twenty years after escaping her own abductor, she still carries the scars—and he was never caught. Now, in the quiet college town of Charlottesville, Virginia, two mothers have vanished on their way to pick up their children from school, leaving behind empty cars and unanswered questions.

While her sister enjoys the picture-perfect life River could never achieve—marriage, children, a beautiful home—River throws herself into the investigation, recognizing patterns that only someone with her traumatic past could see. But as the case intensifies, so do her nightmares, forcing River to confront the darkness she's spent two decades trying to outrun.

With time running out for the missing women and her own past threatening to derail the investigation,

River must decide if facing her demons will be the key to solving the case—or her ultimate undoing.

**1-click River's Edge Now!**

**Read an excerpt from River's Edge on the next page!**

I f you enjoyed this book, please don't forget to leave a review on Amazon and Goodreads! Reviews help me find new readers.

If you have any issues with anything in the book or find any typos, please email me at Kate@kate gable.com. Thank you so much for reading!

## River's Edge Excerpt

There's barely space to move my arms in this conference room.

*Breathe. In, out.* There's nothing inherently bad about being in a tightly crowded space. There is no threat here beyond being forced to smell the onions on the breath of some nearby reporter who needs to practice breathing through their nose. I'm safe.

I wasn't wrong about the media eating this up with a spoon. They're much too transparent. Practically salivating like hungry dogs while we wait for the chief to get started. There's a white screen set up behind a podium and a young uniformed cop fiddles around with a laptop in preparation. There's a lot of murmuring, soft questions, confusion over why this is taking so long to get started.

"Ladies and gentlemen, we're going live in three minutes." The announcement sends a wave of energy through the room, like ripples on an already churning sea. I get my notepad ready, pointedly ignoring the pressing in of bodies on all sides. Charlottesville is a quiet town. Things like this don't happen often here. All the more reason for everybody to jump on a story like this.

It's morbid, but I understand the reason for their eagerness, and it leaves me swallowing back a sense of mild disgust. There's a reason the word vulture is used so often when referring to journalists. They pick every bit of meat off a carcass before posting photos online for everyone to see.

A hush falls over the room when a man some-where between his mid-fifties and early sixties steps up to the podium. He removes his hat, revealing a head of close-cropped gray hair. This is a man who's used to being stressed, strained, the lines on his face a virtual map of the cases he's seen, handled, maybe neglected to close.

His voice is low, gruff, when he begins. "Good evening. Thank you for joining us here for this announcement. We need to make the public aware of the disappearance of two Charlottesville residents at some point today. The timeline is still foggy, but we know for certain these two women dropped their chil-dren off at Shenandoah Elementary this morning, but neglected to pick them up at the usual time. Since then, both women have been out of reach of their loved ones, something which is highly unusual. We are currently tracking their credit card activity and secu-rity footage in the area in hopes of spotting them."

"Tamara Higgins." The image of a woman in her early forties appears on the screen behind Chief Mark

Perkins' head. It looks like she was dressed up for some sort of event, considering her makeup and jewelry. Pretty, with bright blue eyes and hair somewhere between dirty blond and light brown. The camera's flash probably had something to do with that.

"And Beth Clyburn." The image changes, now revealing a petite brunette wearing what looks like workout gear, her hair in a high ponytail, AirPods in her ears. It looks like she just got back from a run and she's glowing, grinning for the photographer.

The captain continues. "This afternoon at approximately three o'clock, the principal of Shenandoah Elementary School placed a call to the spouses of the women in question when their children were not picked up from school and the women's phones went unanswered. Once their husbands were unable to reach them, a call was placed to the police department. Since then, the department has conducted a cursory search of the area and contacted family and friends of these women in hopes of tracking their location, but nothing came of our efforts. It was at that point this was considered an active disappearance."

Watching him, I scribble on my pad without looking at the page. It's something that drives Emma crazy whenever she has to check my notes. "How can you read this chicken scratch?" Like it's not enough for me to be able to read my writing.

*Husbands? Other kids? Friendship, connection?* It does seem strange for two unrelated women to go missing on the same day. I want to know how they knew each other, whether they were close. Could it be a case of women joining forces to leave unhappy situations? Anything could be possible at this point.

"Was there any evidence of a struggle found in either of the homes?" one of the reporters calls out.

The chief's bulldog expression doesn't change. "At this time, we are not going public with details out of an abundance of caution, but we will keep the public posted on any pertinent developments. In the meantime, we ask you all to keep your eyes out for any sign of these two women."

The image changes, now a split screen between the two photos. On the surface, they're very similar. Roughly the same age, pretty, healthy.

Once the conference is over and the room begins to empty, the chief is in my sights. I manage to hold back while he has a quiet conversation with a pair of plainclothes detectives, their badges hanging from lanyards around their necks the way mine does. I make a point of adjusting it now, making sure it's visible. If there's one thing local PD generally doesn't appreciate, it's the presence of the FBI. The way they see it, we're telling them they don't know how to do their jobs. Sadly, that can sometimes be the case.

"Captain Perkins?" I raise a hand to catch the man's attention as he peels away from the detectives.

Immediately, his steely eyes go narrow while the lines already bracketing his mouth deepen in a frown. "Can I help you?"

*Be cordial. You can catch more flies with honey than with vinegar.* The words run through my head as I force a brief, professional smile. "Agent River Collins, sent down from the field office."

He's unimpressed, folding his arms rather than shaking my hand. "We didn't request FBI presence here."

"You might want to take that up with my boss, then, since he sent me down. Special Agent Eric Siwak. I'll give you his number if you would like to call him directly." Easy, easy. Pump the brakes.

Captain Perkins' eyes harden, but it's clear he understands I'm not playing around. He's not going to get me to back down. "What is it I can help you with?" he grunts, sizing me up. Normally, I don't mind being a little on the short side—if anything, I enjoy proving people wrong when they assume I'm a pushover at only a few inches over five feet.

At times like this, though, I find myself standing up straighter, making myself look larger. "For starters, we'd like a little more information on the case. Specifics. I need to get in touch with the husbands, take a look at the homes."

"One thing at a time, Agent." He says it like it's a dirty word, something I should be ashamed of. I notice the looks being shot my way by the local officers who spot me following the chief from the conference room to a small, cluttered office down the hall. He didn't invite me to follow him, but I'm not about to hold my breath and wait.

"The clock is ticking," I remind him once he's behind his desk, heaving a sigh as he opens a folder which I assume holds any information he currently has. "The sooner we can hit the ground running, the better."

I watch, impatient as he heaves a pained sigh once again. "We already have cruisers on the streets, officers going door-to-door in the neighborhood. Nice neighborhood, everybody knows each other."

"So they live in the same neighborhood?"

"Their kids go to the same school, Agent Collins." The man turns sarcasm into an art form. "Yeah, they live in the same neighborhood. Opposite sides, though."

There's a faint ringing in my ears that always accompanies being spoken down to. "What are the spouses saying?"

"What do you think? They don't have the first idea where the wives could be, they've always been reliable, dependable. No problems at home, nothing to hint at any reason to pick up and walk away. The usual."

For these families, this is anything but usual. "Is there anything unusual here? What about the cars? Do we have eyes out for their vehicles?"

"Both vehicles were at their homes."

Interesting. "So there's no saying they ever left to pick up the kids today," I conclude. "They may have left the house, but it wasn't to go to the school."

"It could be," he agrees. "For now, that's the most we can share. The husbands insist their wives would never just, you know, walk out. They don't seem like the type, either," he admits, running a hand over his stubble covered jaw.

"No, they don't," I agree, staring over his shoulder

at the wall behind him but seeing those two women, instead. Bright, sunny smiles. Probably the first to volunteer at school. If they're anything like my sister, they're highly involved in their homes, with their kids. "What are the ages of the children?" I ask as an afterthought.

He looks down at his file. "Tamara Higgins has a nine-year-old daughter and a seven-year-old son. Beth Clyburn has a pair of boys, nine and six."

"So it's not outside the realm of possibility that the two nine-year-olds were in the same class," I muse. "It could tie the women together."

"Plenty of things could tie the women together," he points out. "Now if you'll excuse me, I have a few phone calls to make."

I have been dismissed. Once again, I have to grind my teeth to keep my irritation in check. My emotions are running high, something I can't afford if I want to maintain any semblance of a professional relationship. I might need his help at some point down the line, so it won't do any good to alienate him.

With a tight, professional smile, I murmur, "Thank you for your time. I'll be in touch."

On my way through the door, I hear him grumble behind me. "I don't doubt it."

Pushing it aside, I head straight for the exit. I'm craving a breath of fresh air after being crammed in for so long with so many people. I need to clear my head.

I also need to cool down, to center myself. My hands are shaking as I tuck my notebook in my bag, ghosts of the past are crowding me the way those bodies did in the conference room. This time, there's no hope of getting away from them. I've carried them with me for more than half my life. They aren't going anywhere.

**Want to read more? 1-click River's Edge Now!**

**Forest of Regrets**
**Forest of Deception**

**Detective Charlotte Pierce Psychological**
**Mystery series**
**Last Breath**
**Nameless Girl**
**Missing Lives**
**Girl in the Lake**

# About Kate Gable

Kate Gable loves a good mystery that is full of suspense. She grew up devouring psychological thrillers and crime novels as well as movies, tv shows and true crime.

Her favorite stories are the ones that are centered on families with lots of secrets and lies as well as many twists and turns. Her novels have elements of psychological suspense, thriller, mystery and romance.

Kate Gable lives near Palm Springs, CA with her husband, son, a dog and a cat. She has spent more than twenty years in Southern California and finds inspiration from its cities, canyons, deserts, and small mountain towns.

She graduated from University of Southern California with a Bachelor's degree in Mathematics. After pursuing graduate studies in mathematics, she switched gears and got her MA in Creative Writing and English from Western New Mexico University and her PhD in Education from Old Dominion University.

Writing has always been her passion and obsession. Kate is also a USA Today Bestselling author of romantic suspense under another pen name.

Write her here:

Kate@kategable.com
Check out her books here:
www.kategable.com

Sign up for my newsletter:
https://www.subscribepage.com/kategableviplist

Join my Facebook Group:
https://www.facebook.com/groups/
833851020557518

Bonus Points: Follow me on BookBub and Goodreads!

https://www.bookbub.com/authors/kate-gable

https://www.goodreads.com/author/show/
21534224.Kate_Gable

amazon.com/Kate-Gable/e/B095XFCLL7

facebook.com/KateGableAuthor

bookbub.com/authors/kate-gable

instagram.com/kategablebooks

tiktok.com/@kategablebooks

Printed in Dunstable, United Kingdom